FAKISTS

a novel

John Y. Flanagan

ONION RIVER PRESS

Burlington, Vermont

Onion River Press

47 Maple Street, Suite 214

Burlington, VT 05401

info@onionriverpress.com

www.onionriverpress.com

ISBN: 978-1-957184-22-7

Library of Congress Control Number: 2023902067

To Barb and Vu

ONE

Ruth Landsaw wound an aging Coachmen camper northward along a slim state road. Still frozen pastures spread deep toward the river and chimney smoke curled on the steep wooded hillsides, dissipating above the tree line in the bright and bright blue morning sky. The spring sun wore at patches of lingering snow, the only snow Ruth had seen since trading the oncoming winter for the sun of Casey Key.

She drove the camper out of the farmland and into town, where she crossed the St. George Street Bridge. Abandoned rope swings hung waiting for summer to start.

Ruth parked in the dirt lot at Gary's Market and opened her door to the unsettled air. In Gary's garden, only the waxy heads of hostas suggested new life.

Inside, Gary was standing behind the cigarette counter.

"Ruth Landsaw," he said. "Must be summer."

"It's freezing in here, Gary," she said.

"Keeps the kids awake," Gary said.

He nodded at a cashier hunched over in an insigniated parka with the hood drawn tight.

Ruth mimed a shiver and began to browse for her breakfast, silently assessing the changes Gary had made over the winter. After a few minutes, she brought eggs, frozen English muffins, turkey bacon, and beefsteak tomatoes to the counter. Gary took a small succulent from the gift shelf and placed it on the conveyer belt beside Ruth's items.

"A welcome home for Tom," he said.

Ruth thanked Gary, added the town paper to her pile, and continued in the Coachmen to her small house on the bend in the steep dirt road. Tom Landsaw's '51 Packard was parked with enough room left for Ruth to swing in the camper. In the driveway, Ruth sat for a moment with the engine off and Landsaw emerged from the house in jeans and a ragged flannel. Ruth opened the camper door.

"Gary got you a cactus," she said, sliding down from the captain's chair.

"Weird," Landsaw said. "He got you one, too."

"We'll see which one's nicer and you keep the nice one," she said.

He came over to her and Ruth collapsed into him, and they stood embracing for the first time in the ten years since Landsaw's sentencing.

Landsaw helped Ruth unpack half the camper and begin to settle in. While Ruth sliced the tomatoes, Landsaw filled white teacups painted with pink flowers, pouring dark tea from a matching pot. The wood-stove ticked away with expansion and Rosemary Clooney's "A Hundred Years from Today" spun with intermittent skips and crackles on Ruth's ancient turntable.

"I'll need to take you shopping," Ruth told Landsaw.

"I can shop," Landsaw said, inspecting his sleeves. "You'll need to tell me what the styles are though."

Ruth grunted.

"Like I know," she said. "Just flip through the TV and see what they're all wearing."

Ruth dropped the turkey bacon into a buttered skillet and turned down the burner.

"Did you bring any paintings home?"

Landsaw shook his head.

"That's too bad," she said. "What you showed me was good. You could have had an exhibition, 'Thomas Landsaw: The Prison Years' or something like that."

"I appreciate your readiness for exploitation," Landsaw said.

"It's not exploitation," she said. "Opportunism, maybe."

"Am I still famous?" Landsaw asked.

"Not really," Ruth said. "Maybe in the art world, but I don't pay attention to that."

Landsaw nodded.

"That's good," he said.

He toured the small downstairs rooms and peered out the windows as though he had never looked through them before.

"Who else knows you're home?" Ruth asked from the kitchen.

"Just you," Landsaw said. "And I guess Gary."

"You haven't called anyone?" Ruth asked.

"Who would I call?" Landsaw said. "I don't know anybody anymore."

"I know somebody you know," Ruth said.

Landsaw returned to the kitchen through the small dining room they had rarely used.

"Let's eat," Landsaw said.

"Don't you want to know what she's up to?"

"We wrote," Landsaw said.

"And?"

Landsaw shrugged.

"She's fine."

"Fine where?" Ruth said.

"San Francisco?" Landsaw said.

Ruth's eyebrows raised.

"But you already knew that," he said.

"Just check in," she admitted. "That's all. Sounds like she hates the guy."

"Perceptive," Landsaw said.

He sat down and drew lines out from the ring left by his teacup on the table.

"What does she know?" he asked.

"Not much," Ruth said. "Just that you're out. What else is there to know?"

"Okay," Landsaw said.

"Oh and I did mention that you might be in touch," Ruth added.

"Wonderful," Landsaw said. "An assignment."

"Aren't you curious?" Ruth asked.

"About what?" Landsaw said.

"I don't know," Ruth said. "You were friends."

"We're not the same," Landsaw said.

"People change less than you think."

"Insightful," Landsaw said. "But I don't really feel like revisiting all of that anyway."

"She already knows the story," Ruth said. "You wouldn't even have to tell it."

TWO

Julie White's hometown was called The City of Three Forks, named for the converging of the Jefferson, Gallatin, and Madison Rivers, congregating into the headwaters of the Missouri in Montana. Her family had come from the east, relocating in the early seventies when purchasing remote and expansive tracts of land was a popular thing to do. Her uncles had spread out upstate and into Vermont, and so it was incumbent upon Julie's father to settle into wilder territory, farther west.

When the time had come for college, and with family still planted in New York and New England, Julie had little trouble selling her lapsed Catholic parents on Saint Bartholomew's, a small art school on the western banks of Lake Placid, with vague roots to a since forgotten clergy. Her parents were pacified knowing that family would be nearby if trouble found her, though trouble tended not to find Julie. She possessed an easiness endorsed by her intelligence, one that she was not apt to be boastful of, and she was beautiful in way that was not obvious. In high school, where any discernable attribute would be game for ridicule, the only charge her classmates could find to level against her was her self-possession. She developed a proclivity for watercolors and painted the landscapes that cradled her world, the backgrounds into which she could withdraw completely or simply regard from a distance at her choosing.

It was the winter of her freshman year when Julie's "New Masters" class at St. Bart's was assigned to visit the Beaumont Museum, a massive marble anomaly in the otherwise modest town surrounding the college. Julie had been sitting close enough to Landsaw when their professor, an avuncular adjunct who wore his adopted career like an ill-fitting sweater, encouraged those with cars to offer rides to those without.

Landsaw had painted, too, though where Julie had developed her medium gradually, Landsaw had been encouraged to suppress his. Working in oils, with the occasional default into acrylics, his craft was to copy existing works. He painted renowned masterpieces with an undeniable exactness, which had been obvious from his earliest days. In grammar school, he would sketch the slides projected in art class with a hand that seemed guided by a grace he doubted. Word of the admiration he received from his teachers had made it home to other parents, and one day the praise ceased abruptly.

By high school, though, his talent was prodigious enough to warrant a scholarship into an exchange program in Verona. No Italian students were interested in spending a semester enduring a winter in Vermont, and so Landsaw was exchanged for no one. When he returned, the state's biggest paper dubbed him a "Green Mountain Michelangelo," a sobriquet that would further ostracize him from his classmates. To Landsaw, the social costs of talent were never worth the ever-diminishing returns. At St. Bart's he had found little to reignite his interest in anything at all until Julie White opened his passenger-side door.

"Cool car," she said. "What is it?"

"A Packard?" Landsaw said. "'51."

"That's old," she said.

"Not too old," he said. "40-something?"

He had already started the car but tried to start it again, hoping Julie had not noticed.

"Where'd you get it?" she asked.

"My dad," he said. "Well I mean it was his and then he died and now it's mine."

"Cool," Julie said. "I mean, holy shit, I'm so sorry."

"It's cool," Landsaw said. "I mean the car is cool."

The Beaumont was on the main road demarcating the north boundary of the small downtown. The drive from campus was short and direct, though Landsaw extended it with a circuitous route. The exhibition they were assigned to visit was that of a critically trending Irish painter named Lorcan Lang. Lang was an abstract painter, scheduled to arrive on the St. Bart's campus as a teaching artist in residence the following semester.

At the museum, Julie and Landsaw discovered that the majority of Lang's canvases were a sturdy block of unmixed color, swathed on and abandoned, raw in the style of an already-dated era. A photograph of Lang hung on the gallery wall. In it, the artist stood among his canvases in a high-ceilinged studio. He looked away from the camera, inhaling a cigarette in black and white. Landsaw hurried past each painting as though the assignment had been merely to count them. Distinctly, Julie tended to each of them like a bee upon blossoms, absorbing every one in sequence. When she was finished, she found Landsaw reading a skydiving pamphlet from the brochure rack in the lobby.

"You finished quickly," she said.

"The first one finished me," he said.

"Yeah," she said. "I guess they're just kind of whatever."

Julie and Landsaw walked out through a heavy double doorway and into a light snow.

"Thick paint, thin concept," Julie said.

"They just pissed me off," Landsaw said.

"Articulate," Julie said. "At least they provoked something in you, I guess?"

"So do people who blow their noses in restaurants," he said.

They got into the Packard and Landsaw pulled out into the street.

"So what do you paint?" Julie asked.

"Other paintings mostly," he said. "You know like copyists do? Those people who sit in museums all day and recreate something that already exists, but worse? I don't do it much anymore. How about you?"

"Just landscapes," Julie said. "Generally. In watercolor. Is that rewarding, painting other paintings?"

"Sort of," Landsaw said. "Sometimes."

He was taking the short way back but he was taking it slowly.

"It sort of seems like it wouldn't be," Julie said. "I mean no offense. I obviously don't know."

"Are landscapes rewarding?" Landsaw asked.

"When they're good they are," she said.

"What's the difference then?" he said. "Both of us copy something that's already there, right?"

Julie watched out the window as Landsaw took a sweeping curve at the crest of the hill that the campus claimed the top of. An enormous lake view framed the red brick buildings and snow-covered evergreens.

"I guess I can change my referents to be however I want them to be," Julie said. "And that's sort of the point. Like there aren't really any formal rules or anything. While you have to make something into what it is already, as much as possible."

"I guess," Landsaw said. "But there's definitely some reward in that constraint."

"Hm," Julie said.

"Anyway, where to next?" Landsaw tried.

"Oh," Julie said and paused. "I promised someone I'd meet them."

"Sounds serious," Landsaw said. "Guess I better step on it."

He caught Julie smiling slightly as he turned back into the parking lot. When he pulled up to the dormitory, he wondered if getting out to open Julie's door for her would be a strange thing to do. He decided that it would be, and pretended to adjust the radio while Julie unbuckled her seat belt and opened her own door. She stood up out of the Packard.

"Tell someone hi?" Landsaw said.

Julie ducked down and looked at Landsaw, her smile now in earnest, before closing the door.

THREE

Ron Paquette was Ruth and Landsaw's closest neighbor; a stand-in, too, for when Ruth was too exhausted by the demands of single parenting and needed a partner whom she did not have to live with. A bachelor whose string of unserious boyfriends traced well beyond county lines, Ron filled the role readily, performing a vaunted duty while remaining inculpable from any consequence his influence might have had on the boy, a privilege Ruth could never know. Ron owned a private swim and tennis club just beyond Burlington, an inheritance from his father. He taught tennis, drank at the bar, chain-smoked on his riding mower, harassed the ever-graduating stable of jock lifeguards, and collected and dispensed dirt on the local gentry. The primal upkeep of the grounds spoke for his resentment as caretaker. The glassware was mismatched, the ballroom parquet had warped and become moldy, and the vending machines, inflicted with grounding woes, hummed ceaselessly. The dated atmosphere hung in the balance between vintage and destitution. But it was popular nonetheless among those who had been raised in the outposts of wealthier cities and expected the same manufactured exclusivity wherever they went in life.

Among this set were the Fiores, whose son would have been Landsaw's age had he not drowned at a summer camp. When Ron had first hired Landsaw to work the bar in high school, the couple issued uncomfortable comparisons regularly between him and their departed son, supposing in greater depth with each drink what he might have achieved.

The majority of Ron's clientele preferred the dark and air-conditioned bar to the sunny poolside patio. For parties and rentals, Landsaw was an amenity: ears, eyes, and arms to be employed at the guests' disposal. His preferred station was valet, where he was able to drive expensive cars at concerning speeds.

One midsummer Saturday night, when the Saint Bartholomew's board of directors had rented Ron's club for a fundraiser, a keg kicked and Landsaw went to change it. He passed the tired blues band stirring up the septuagenarians who danced like zombies, clapping sinewy arms and shuffling sinewy legs in their own miscued rhythms beneath the borrowed chandelier in the oversize tent. He curled through the kitchen toward the walk-in refrigerator, spirited by the reprieve of a cold beer for himself. His hand was on the handle when he heard the unmistakable pants of pleasure coming from behind the insulated door. He knocked twice and the noises stopped. Landsaw pantomimed retreating to the kitchen with clomping footsteps diminishing in heft, providing the couple with a moment to clear out uncaught. But assuming Landsaw had simply gone away, the lovers resumed. Again Landsaw knocked, and soon a woman wearing makeup that registered to Landsaw as raccoon-like opened the door and slid out, reconstituting her party dress as she disappeared past him with a curious smile. Landsaw opened the door wider and discovered a man with a graying fuzz of hair, buckling his belt. The man turned to look at Landsaw.

"Don't mind me," he said.

He finished with his pants and came to meet Landsaw in the doorway.

"Jim Rolando," the man said.

Jim Rolando stuck out his hand for Landsaw to shake.

Landsaw looked at Rolando's hand and then again at his face.

"Oh right," Rolando said, withdrawing the gesture.

He wore rimless glasses and had an imperfect Van Dyke that Landsaw guessed to be a summer experiment.

"I need to change a keg," Landsaw said. "Sorry to interrupt."

"Not at all," Rolando said. "Just finishing up. Which one is it?"

Rolando turned toward and scanned the double stack of half-kegs lining the walls. Landsaw followed, allowing the door to close behind them. He found the empty barrel and twisted off its tap and coil.

"Hey," Rolando said, sizing up the cases of beer along the far wall. "Think I might have one of these? I'll bet the line out there is still a motherfucker."

Landsaw plucked two beers from an open case and handed one to Rolando.

"Thanks," Rolando said. "So you in school around here?"

Landsaw punctured a fresh keg with the tap and locked it in place.

"High school," he said. "But I'm—"

"The painter!" Rolando said.

He aimed an index finger at Landsaw.

"You're the painter! You just went to France or Italy or something. I read about you. The paper said you're really something. Hey, remind me what grade you're going to be in next year?"

"Senior," Landsaw said.

"And where will you go to school after that?"

"I might not," Landsaw said.

"Uh oh," Rolando said. "Gotta go to school, Michelangelo. Even artists go to college."

"Then I guess I'm still deciding," Landsaw said.

"Ever seen St. Bart's?" Rolando asked.

Landsaw said he had not.

"Oh it's nice," Rolando said. "Real nice. Right over by Lake Placid, in New York. And the art program is just terrific. I don't know if you've looked into it already. Art at Bart? Really making a national name for itself."

Landsaw sipped his beer and thought about how he might leave Jim Rolando.

"In fact," Rolando said, "If you can keep this little walk-in walk-in under your hat, I bet we could arrange a tour of the campus. Maybe see what it would take to get you in up there. No promises or anything. How does that sound?"

Landsaw didn't know how it sounded, but he told Rolando that it sounded good.

"Well great," Rolando said. "Been a pleasure meeting you and everything, but let's vamoose. I'm freezing my dick off."

When the bar phone at Ron's club rang a few days later, Landsaw discovered Rolando on the line.

"This that Landsaw?" he asked.

"Yes sir," Landsaw said.

"Jim Rolando, Tom," Rolando said. "How we doing?"

Landsaw began to answer but Rolando cut him off.

"Anyway I just wanted to say that I wasn't bullshitting the other night. I really do think you'd enjoy taking a look at what they're doing over there with the Art at Bart program. Some really exciting opportunities. World class. It's a tremendous place. And with your Europe credentials, I really think you'd excel."

Later that week Landsaw was standing on the lush greenery of the St. Bart's campus with Ruth and Jim Rolando, who Landsaw had learned chaired the St. Bart's board. Rolando was wearing sunglasses and beaming at the manicured splendor surrounding them. Ruth was beaming, too, and Landsaw thought only of her when he accepted Rolando's generous scholarship. Privately, he wondered if a library card might not provide an equally comprehensive education against anything he might learn at the college. He revisited this thought two years later, watching Julie fumble with the keys to her dormitory. He was suddenly convinced she was the most achingly intriguing person on campus, and more than he resented her implausible appointment, he resented his inability to divert her from it.

FOUR

Once an importing tycoon's far-flung country retreat, the large estate set back off the main road from campus was falling into dilapidation. Paint peeled from its balustrades and the roof released more scalloped shingles into the overgrown yard each year. Legends formed around it: the house where the young wife went mad; where the baby died; where the first dean hung himself. One rumor claimed that the half-charred remains of a student's botched suicide had been too gruesome to clean up, and that the house was padlocked and abandoned with the mess still inside. Landsaw gave no credence to these tales, though he did find credible the one about the paper-skinned junky living in the basement. And so he was nonplussed when the address listed for his new elective course matched the numbers engraved into the brick entry columns at the apron of the mansion's long drive.

The vaguely titled "Elements of Design" class was among those the college offered as credit-rich night courses in which students taught other students, removing the professor, and their requisite salary, from the traditional equation. It was a popular sell on campus tours, with parents too enthralled by the newly erected student center, which students rarely used, to identify this cost-cutting measure for what it was.

Landsaw navigated the ice-slick driveway and approached the house, discovering the lower level lit with an inviting glow against the oncoming night. A porch light suggested the expectation of his arrival. As he took the steps, a support post for the railing danced out from its holding and the whole unit wobbled under the suggestion of his weight. He guided the post back into its vacancy and continued on unassisted, carrying the plastic grocery bag containing the charcoals and sketchpad listed on the syllabus that he had received in the campus mail. He did not carry with him the idea for a project that was also listed on the syllabus. He had planned to come up with something on the walk over, but had become distracted by the full and straw-colored moon rising to the east over the freezing lake. He knocked on the glass window of the old oak door and waited. Soon, the sound of feet hurried down the hallway and a silhouette appeared behind the window's lace curtain. The door opened with Julie behind it.

"Hey it's you," she said.

"And you," Landsaw said. "You're taking this class, too?"

"I'm teaching it," she said. "But you're taking this class. The only one, actually. I didn't know your last name. Landsaw? What is that, English?"

Landsaw composed himself.

"We think it's Czech," he said. "But aren't sure. Maybe Bohemian?"

"Like the song," Julie said.

"'Musetta's Waltz?'" Landsaw asked.

"What?" Julie said. "No. Here, come in."

The inside of the house was warm and significantly less destitute than its exterior. The essence of recent carpentry still lingered.

Julie led Landsaw into what had been the dining room, where she had laid out her own drawing pad and pencils. She had also set out pretzel twists in a plastic bowl.

"I'm really the only one?" Landsaw asked.

He laid his shopping bag on the table.

"Yup," she said. "I guess most students prefer to be taught by like actual teachers."

"What's up with this place anyway?" he asked. "Don't ghosts or murderous addicts live here or something?"

"I hope not," Julie said. "But if they do I haven't seen them. I think the college wanted to use it for events and stuff, but ran out of money after refinishing the inside. Or something like that. It's massive in here. And this feels ridiculous."

She gestured toward their things on the table.

"What does?" Landsaw said.

"I was sort of expecting to teach someone who doesn't already know what they're doing. Like someone who doesn't care and just wanted to take this because it was easy."

"But that is why I'm taking it," Landsaw said. "I genuinely don't care. I'll prove that quickly."

"Did you bring an idea with you?" Julie asked. "Something to work on? I guess we could go over that."

"I did," Landsaw said. "Definitely."

"Alright," Julie said. "What is it?"

Landsaw reached for a pretzel twist.

"Where are you from again?" he asked.

"Montana?" Julie said, as though Landsaw might not have heard of it. "What about you?"

"Vermont," he said.

Intending to point east, he pointed south.

"Is Montana cold like it is here? I mean now, in winter?"

"Not quite so cold," Julie said. "Half the snow where I am. Bigger mountains."

"What made you come here?" Landsaw asked. "I mean the cold is kind of awful, isn't it? The wind and everything freezing your nose hairs. And the summers are about three weeks long. The mountains are nice, but it sounds like the mountains in Montana are maybe nicer? The lake is good, too. Farms and everything. And lots of forests to walk around in, I guess. But there are probably forests in Montana? I mean I'm assuming."

Julie looked at Landsaw.

"I think I lost you there," she said. "Are you asking if there are forests in Montana?"

"I didn't intend to," Landsaw said, "but I think that's what I did."

"There are," Julie said. "Why I came here, since I think that's what you started to ask, was to study art and to be somewhere unfamiliar, away from home."

"Are you satisfied?" he asked "With the intergalactically renowned Art at Bart program, I mean?"

"So far no," Julie admitted. "I sort of feel duped."

"Duped how?" he asked. "I mean, me too, but I wonder if we feel duped in the same way."

"Just by what they were selling versus what it is, I guess? Like this. Neither of us are getting anything out of this, right? I can't teach you anything."

"You probably could," Landsaw said.

"It's so ridiculous," Julie said.

Landsaw sensed she was on the verge of acute disquiet and he looked around the room for a diversion. Lifeless landscapes hung on the wall beside built-in bookshelves stuffed with board games instead of books.

"Let's play one of those for now," Landsaw said. "I don't feel much like drawing."

"As long as you don't report me or something," Julie said. "Sure."

"And I get an automatic A," Landsaw said.

"I didn't say that," Julie said. "Let's play *Sorry!*"

Throughout the game, Julie split her sevens, used her fours to go home backwards, saved her final pawn at the start to wait on the *Sorry!* card, and slowed the game to a crawl whenever Landsaw pushed ahead, performing every move in capitulation to the nature of the game. Landsaw stumbled through a strategy he had devised at the onset and neglected to revise. In the end, Julie destroyed him.

"Loser picks the next game," she said.

Landsaw chose *Battleship*.

"Less strategy in this one," he said.

Julie said nothing, and after winning easily, she asked if he cared to try *Stratego*.

"Not much strategy there, either," she said.

"I give up," Landsaw said. "More of a *Twister* guy I guess."

"We're probably good for tonight," Julie said. "Should we try to do some actual work next time? Thursday I think?"

"Sure," Landsaw said. "I'll actually bring an idea."

By Thursday, Landsaw had still failed to generate any sense of inspiration for a project with Julie, but he was encouraged to discover that Julie did not mind.

Landsaw brought in wood from the collapsed pile beneath the porch and lit a fire in the fireplace. He had borrowed a bottle of wine from his roommate but neglected to bring a corkscrew. He dug out the cork with a steak knife and he and Julie drank the wine from plastic green cups that tasted like dish soap. After a few minutes, Julie asked Landsaw if the smoke engulfing the downstairs rooms was normal, and Landsaw rushed

19

to open the flue. He singed his sleeve slightly and Julie went to open the windows. The flames in the hearth swelled to a healthy burn, but the outside cold overwhelmed their negligible heat.

"How long do those need to be open?" she asked Landsaw.

"I don't know," he said. "Not long."

"I think there are blankets upstairs," Julie said. "I'll get one."

Soon Landsaw and Julie were huddled together beneath a quilt before the fire. The bad wine emboldening him, Landsaw's hand explored to Julie's, and he was relieved when she pivoted and sank into him. They stayed that way for as long as they could, until the cold became unbearable, and Landsaw got up to close the windows. When he returned, Julie was on the couch beneath the blanket, her clothes in a crumple on the floor. They were clumsy beneath the quilt until they discovered a common rhythm, though with great difficulty, they braked before the commitment that they agreed, without saying so, would spoil their yet-settled beginning.

FIVE

Winter lingered, lifting into spring only as the semester closed and final exams required more attention than the students were willing to give them. Even the most committed of artists-in-training could not help but dismiss their work to go outside. The vernal buzz opened windows to freshen the stale soup of dormitory air. Grass was green again and sun streaked the campus lawns in light that stretched the shadows to monstrous lengths. Bare skin came back to flatter curiously similar styles, and Landsaw wondered if there had not been conspiring among a secret legion of tastemakers worldwide to decide what everyone would wear come spring.

Summer was a prospect with bittersweet reprieve. Landsaw doubted the nascent sketch of the relationship he and Julie had conjured could survive the span of a three-month pause. Montana might as well have been the moon.

Julie had promised Landsaw an off-campus adventure before the break, and Landsaw let her drive the Packard to the trailhead of a ridge-spanning hike. Buds covered the tree limbs on the Adirondack foothills. Landsaw and Julie parked in the small lot, checking their packs and working their feet into hiking boots still stiff from winter. There was an hour of light left when they reached the summit campsite. This time Julie built the fire, with brush and curls of dry birch and pared branches from fallen pines to work up a dependable flame. Landsaw brought over two beers from his pack.

"You know how coyotes eat dogs?" Julie asked him.

"Do I know that coyotes eat dogs?" Landsaw said. "Or are you asking if I know the steps a coyote takes to eat a dog?"

"More the latter," she said.

She popped the top of the beer Landsaw had handed her and slurped at the froth that flooded the rim.

"I heard the pack sends the youngest coyote out to play with the dog," she said. "To engage it or something and build trust."

"My neighbor's dog ate a coyote once actually," Landsaw said.

"Wow," Julie said. "Well anyway, I guess the coyote sends the youngest out to make friends with the dog and tries to get the dog to chase it, which isn't that hard because it's a dog and it loves to chase shit."

"Not our dog," Landsaw said. "The one we had? It only had three legs and wasn't very fast. Our neighbor Ron found it in a trailer one time after the owner had died in the bathtub. I guess it was super gross. The body had expanded to the size of the tub and was all purple and oozing. Like really, really gross."

"I'm trying to tell you something, Landsaw," Julie said.

"Right," he said. "Sorry."

"I was saying that when the little coyote gets the dog to chase it, it leads the dog over to where the big coyotes are waiting in a big circle that the dog can't see. The little coyote and the dog keep playing, and while they're playing, the circle gets smaller and smaller until eventually the first coyote walks away and the dog is all alone in the middle of these big coyotes closing in, and it knows it's fucked."

"Vicious," Landsaw said.

He popped his beer can open. The sun was now barely there in the distance, just a faint slice of orange sinking into the dark mountains.

"Are you telling me you're going to kill me?" Landsaw asked.

"I might," Julie said. "I'm just saying that I like to see everything at once. With anything. The whole pack now, you know?"

Landsaw poked at the fire with the branch he had designated as the branch with which to poke the fire.

"I don't think you can," he said. "Like with anything, or most things. I mean how would you? Things aren't set up like that, I don't think."

Julie trained her eyes on the flames snapping out at them.

"I guess I just mean no tricks," she said.

"You mean with me?" he said.

"With anything," she said. "But yeah with you."

Landsaw agreed and Julie climbed into her sleeping bag. She leaned on Landsaw, and whenever the smoke found their faces, they both closed their eyes.

SIX

Sunny Shimura was on the wrong coast for surfing. Americans who had visited his native Tokyo had shared with him some of the finest stateside breaks—Queen of the Coast, First Point, Secos, and Zuma—but he found none of these waves on the east, where he had landed for what appeared to be a promising career in the field of forensics. The specialty he had selected, on little more than a whim, was art crime.

When he had first moved to the U.S., in the late 1960s, the art scene in Los Angeles was just gaining traction, and for the time being, anyone working in the business of detecting fakes and forgeries was all but required to station themselves along the wave-challenged shores along the north Atlantic seaboard. From his South Shore perch on Pemigewasset Point, an industrial outpost near Quincy, he sought waves he had heard rumored to exist, but aside from a few storm-induced squalls, rarely was the surfing worth the wetsuit. He awoke before light on even the most unforgiving of winter mornings to paddle out, despite often finding chop not even large enough to stand on. But he relished the solitude nonetheless. Oceanside dwellers in parkas walked condo-sized dogs and watched

Sunny far out on the horizon, sitting with the seagulls in the rain and snow.

He was similarly regarded at work. Both the FBI and the Museum of Fine Art co-signed his paychecks, and the bicameral nature of his position meant that both pillars of Sunny's profession distrusted him equally, and intensely. His focus on art bought him scant credibility among the homicide detectives on the law enforcement limb of his duties, and being a cop sicced on the scrutiny of art assured Sunny permanent ostracization from his peers at the museum. Furthermore, his museum coworkers took offense to the binary approach to which Sunny was required to interpret artworks: real, or fake. Beyond questions of authorship, Sunny earned no accolades from the museum's director for proving that a batch of Vlamincks won at auction for no small expense were in fact the worthless fakes of an Ibizan hustler. His office was situated in the basement of the MFA, beside the on-site laundry. The room reeked of the detergents and dyes used to bleach the gala linens back to white. His space was simple, with few personal embellishments, and he organized his files impeccably.

One summer day, after a typically flat morning on the water, Sunny was unloading his surfboard from the luggage rack of his blue Mercedes diesel when his landlord, Mrs. Owens, likewise his downstairs neighbor, signaled for his attention. Mrs. Owens was an increasingly unhinged shut-in who had lived in her duplex apartment since being born there. Maverick cigarettes and the fretful eyes of near-constant drinking made her look fathoms closer to the grave than her age would suggest. Sunny approached her porch. Mrs. Owens was sitting in a vinyl lawn chair smoking in an elaborately patterned nightdress.

"Someone come looking for you," she told Sunny.

"Who?" Sunny asked.

Mrs. Owens reached into a pocket and showed Sunny a slip of paper.

"Can't say," she said. "He don't leave a name. Just this."

She handed Sunny the paper. On it was a scribbled phone number and nothing else.

"Had an accent," Mrs. Owens said. "He was ugly, I thought. And old. Scared the heck outta Natalie."

Behind the porch window, Natalie, Mrs. Owens' Lhasa Apso, barked, as she did incessantly.

"What kind of accent?" Sunny asked.

"Oh who the heck knows," Mrs. Owens said. "These days could be anything. You're the goddam detective."

Mrs. Owens snubbed out her cigarette and reached for the pack on the glass patio table beside her. Sunny said thanks and returned to unloading his car. After carrying his board up the outside stairs to the sagging second-story porch where he kept it, he called the number. A voice inflected by an accent Sunny recognized unmistakably as deeply Southern American traveled through the line.

C. Blake Steward had cut himself loose from the highbred Mississippi stock he had been born into. He had leveraged the Seward name to avoid the Second World War and to earn entrance into Harvard Divinity, where he stopped attending classes following his freshman year, upon discovering himself an agnostic. He remained enrolled to appease the draft board and stayed on in Cambridge after college, making rent by selling popcorn at the Battenkill movie theater, on Battenkill Street. But as fortune tends to find those ill-equipped to manage it, one night, while using a mirror to fix a faulty transmitter on his RCA, Seward stumbled into inventing the early circuitry that would become the color television. He had no use for the millions that came quickly, and so he bought the Battenkill. Even as owner, Seward was not above selling tickets and jerking sodas to move the lines along. He was exacting about few things, but at Seward's Battenkill, the films always ran on time.

Slowly at first, Seward busied the blank Corinthian blue walls of his Cambridge loft with extravagant artworks that followed no discernable pattern of taste. He claimed to converse with each artifact, allowing the frames to engulf his interior life entirely. By the time Sunny arrived at Seward's home, decades after the first piece had been fastened to the wall, his collection numbered in the thousands.

"I've spent a good deal of my life convincing myself that I am not obsessed," he told Sunny when they met at the apartment.

Though Seward had left the south, its sense of decorum had not left him. He dressed impeccably, and despite welcoming few visitors to his rooms, as Sunny guessed he did, Seward executed the finest points of etiquette with comforting ease. His slow gait betrayed his seven decades as he walked Sunny through the collection. With no more than a flutter of a hand at each, Seward strolled by Goyas, Turners, early Singer Sargents, sculptures by Henry Moore and Edith Woodman Burroughs. His modernist wing included a stunning retrospective: Gauguin; Pollock; Matisse; Van Gogh; and Renoir. He provided Sunny with brief histories of his acquisitions. But as he spoke, Sunny sensed a tone of despair, and he began to theorize that the peculiar collector was feeling remorse for spending his fortune on accumulating objects specific to his personal pleasure. But when they entered the central room of Seward's cavernous collection, Sunny discovered the spring of the millionaire's anxiety. On a pedestal bolted to the ground stood the Housemann *Bottom*, immediately recognizable to Sunny, as it would have been to anyone with even the most remote interest in art history. It was among the most famous of stolen artifacts, a marble sculpture of Shakespeare's donkey-headed weaver, cast by the Boston-born Neoclassicist Henrietta Housemann, whose name held astronomically high regard among east coast collectors. Seward displayed no other works in the large, dark room, allowing the figure to reign with a dizzying presence in its strange mélange of comic breeziness and classical stoicism. Sunny turned to Seward to discover the aged collector wearing a complex expression of rapture peering out through pain.

"I never wanted it," he told Sunny. "I still don't."

"It would be discourteous of me not to advise you to find a lawyer before you continue," Sunny said.

Seward waved him off. "I don't want a lawyer," he said. "I'm too tired for any of that. I just want it out of here."

Housemann had presented the sculpture as a centennial birthday gift to Boston's extravagant Boylston Theatre, the city's grand palace of the performing arts. The statue's arrival was a press sensation, having made the voyage from the artist's studio in Rome to the banks of the Charles River before its installation on the landing of the grand staircase in the theater's main lobby. It was beloved for decades, until one morning, when a box office agent arriving at work discovered that the Housemann was gone. The famous case never produced a promising lead.

"It was a gift," Seward told Sunny. "He moved it here to surprise me, and it really was a surprise. He told me it was an early test casting or something like that, but then of course the papers came. I don't know how he thought I wouldn't know, and I was so sick I couldn't confront him. But it turned out I didn't have to, because suddenly he was gone."

Sunny watched Seward closely, reading his expression for betrayals of performance.

"Some gift," Sunny said. "With the right attorney you might arrange an anonymous return, but not without sharing who gave it to you."

"That I cannot do, Detective Shimura," Seward said.

Sunny watched Seward closely.

"Mr. Seward," Sunny said. "Why did you find me?"

"You're not regular police," Seward said. "You understand art, don't you?"

"This doesn't go away without a name," Sunny said.

Seward shook his head.

"Beyond that," Seward said, "What is your advice to me, detective?"

"Call regular police," Sunny said.

SEVEN

Lorcan Lang came to. The room was black but for a digital clock face blurred through the smear of sleep. The phone rang loudly and another figure stirred in the covers beside him, turning on her side toward Lang. Lang picked up the phone and put it back down. His hangover hit before his feet were out from the snarl of sheets and onto the hotel room carpet. He peeled his clothes from the floor and tried to make out the face of his companion. Having driven down from Donegal and beginning the night at a pub with the few friends he had left in Dublin, he had apparently made a new one. A shower would have woken her. He eased into his blazer, tapping for and finding his passport in its left breast pocket.

The shuttle was empty but for Lang and the driver. Lang watched the wet road as it passed out the window and he felt his eyes sink into his face. His chest ached with the parchment of booze-bruised innards. At the airport he wheeled his bag behind him to the counter, where he withdrew from it a folder with the contact information for the new colleague he would be staying with in New York. He had accepted the temporary teaching job at Saint Bartholomew's out of desperation, but now his career was gaining traction and he regretted the commitment severely. He had tried to leverage his nascent renown to demand his own apartment, but the administration had refused, and when he threatened to back out, they reminded Lang of the contract he did not remember signing, stipulating the financial penalties he would incur for jumping ship.

Lang purchased a newspaper and a muffin from a café near his gate before finding a phone and pecking in the number.

"Professor Lang?" the voice on the other end said.

"Well," Lang said. "Lorcan, yes. And you're John then."

"Great to hear from you," John Pond said. "You're at the airport?"

"In Dublin still," Lang said.

Pond paused as though Lang had more to say.

"Marvelous," Pond said finally. "There's a number I can call to track your flights, so I'll be there when you land."

"Wonderful," Lang said. "Thank you."

"You're coming through the city, is that right?"

"New York City," Lang said. "Yes."

For a moment Lang lost himself in the sleepless metropolis that might have been his final destination had the critical gentry discovered him earlier, rather than the rural outpost hours north where he would endure a cold and isolated winter. He despised St. Bart's already.

"Terrific," Pond said. "This is really going to be a lot of fun."

"Indubitably," Lang said before hanging up.

He threw the muffin away untried and made an attempt at divining significance from the same few lines of vibrating newsprint until his flight was called. He puked on the plane and fell asleep, with the paper folded on his lap. The passenger beside him was an older guy named Guy, who told Lang how he had been visiting Ireland to watch his grandson play soccer. Lang hoped his grunts at Guy's enumerations of what he had seen on his trip registered at least as indifference, but it took his vomiting, the eruption of which began in his seat, to finally snuff out their discourse.

Lang found JFK to be much like the Dublin Airport, except that it was larger and its stores sold Statue of Liberty and taxicab tchotchkes instead of shamrock gewgaws and pennywhistles. His body demanded alcohol, and he reasoned that the booze on his breath could be excused if it were fresh from lunch. At a sports bar, he watched American television, a cycle of weather and ultimately inconsequential crises. At the second airport after his quick second flight, Lang spotted the man who must have been John Pond in the baggage carousel. Pond held a hand-rendered sign that read PROFESSOR LANG, along with a crimson and navy Saint Bartholomew's pennant.

"Lorcan!" Pond called.

They walked together to the parking lot. Where Lang had expected crisp leaves and biting wind, summer heat still steamed off the pavement and resplendent trees held their bloom along the roads. The Ponds' house was set on a small street spanning a high bank along the lake. Views of the sharply blue water and dim mountains filled the generous gaps between the houses. Pond pulled into the driveway of his two-story bungalow.

"That's Frances, my wife," he told Lang as he climbed out from the car.

Frances walked down from the screened-in porch and crossed the small lawn and gravel drive in her bare feet to greet them.

"You made it," she told Lang, and then she laughed as though it would have been ridiculous had he not.

Pond hefted Lang's suitcase out of the car and traced Frances' steps back to the porch with it.

"Good enough for now," Pond said. "We can do the tour later, unless you're antsy for it now."

"Not quite," Lang said.

"Good," Pond said. "Then I say it's cocktail hour."

The visiting professor hoped he wasn't beaming too brightly.

EIGHT

Lang struggled with the heavy door to Hart Hall while negotiating his leather bag with the broken shoulder strap, weak coffee spilling from the Spirit of St. Louis mug that Pond had insisted he take for his office. Students filed through the hallways with somnambulistic automation. Their shoes squealed from the outside rain. Lang was only half hungover, though the three-story climb to his office elicited temporary dominance of the queasier half. He found his door, which was directly beside Pond's own. The office itself was comfortable enough, though he would request that the college find him a couch and maybe a rug to cover the uninspiring brown of the wall-to-wall.

The art studios were on the first floor and on the opposite side of the building from his office. The trek there required navigation through a long and congested annex. Timing himself, the trip took Lang four minutes. The studio, he thought, looked more like a storage space. Mannequins, easels, some broken, some not, plastic apples and pears, paintbrushes protruding from denuded paint cans, brass urns unpolished, and paint-soiled drop cloths littered the spacious room. Desks with drafting planes were jammed into a crooked circle and an unignorable hum droned from the tangle of HVAC machinery bolted to the curiously tall ceiling.

On the first day of classes, Lang found the American students less incompetent than he had expected. The more sycophantic of the bunch even knew who he was. Julie sat next to Landsaw. By the end of the class, each of them had worked out a passable imitation of Lang's Irish patter, a rendering that would only improve in time.

"Tissis de paintbroosh," Landsaw exclaimed as he walked with Julie back to his new off-campus apartment.

"An dis," Julie added, "De fookin paint."

"What a boob," Landsaw said. "How scotched was he? I don't think I can stand a whole semester with that cartoon idiot."

"Idjit," Julie corrected.

"Saw him breathe his booze breath on you," Landsaw said.

"He already touched my shoulder for a weird amount of time," Julie said.

"Saw that, too," Landsaw said.

"I am kind of starting to like his paintings more now though," Julie said.

"Pictures," Landsaw said. "Pichers."

"What?" Julie said.

"He calls them 'pictures,'" Landsaw said. "He doesn't call them 'paintings.' The wall at the gallery said that, remember? He calls paintings 'pictures' because he thinks 'paintings' puts too much historical weight on them, or something. With 'pictures' I guess he gets out of that."

"Or he's just making it worse," Julie said.

They arrived at the apartment on a tree-lined street with once-fine houses now made derelict by years of student abuse. None of the loose acquaintances Landsaw was living with were home, and Landsaw and Julie went upstairs to fill the bright afternoon with a bygone summer's worth of unchecked entanglement.

In the onset of night, Julie left and Landsaw readied his books for the library, where he was planning to meet his friend Jagger. During his freshman year at St. Bart's, Landsaw had befriended Paul Wood, whom everybody called Jagger on account of his suggestive pout, moony eyes, and outré mop of feathered hair. Though Jagger had come from Connecticut, he spoke in a flat New York accent that Landsaw suspected his friend exaggerated in order to distinguish himself from the rest of the student body, many of who spoke in the crude bark of a New England drawl. Jagger greeted him with a flask of rum that tasted more like the flask than it did of rum.

"What do you have to work on?" Jagger asked Landsaw.

Landsaw told Jagger that his assignment from Lang was to find lines in the real world and turn them into *artistic* lines.

"Artistic lines?" Jagger asked.

"His term," Landsaw said. "Not mine."

"What the fuck does that even mean?" Jagger said.

"I think he just means lines," Landsaw said.

"I have to read 200 pages of *Bleak House* and write a 2,000-word essay about it, and you have to draw a fucking a line."

"But it has to be an *artistic* line," Landsaw corrected.

Jagger took his pen and scribbled on the back of his hand.

"There," he said.

"But it's on your hand," Landsaw said, "which is still in the real world, not the artistic world."

Jagger pressed his hand to a blank notebook page, leaving a smudge.

"There," he said again.

"Not a line," Landsaw said. "That's a smudge."

"It's my interpretation of a line," Jagger said. "It was a line and now it's a smudge representing a line that no longer exists. It's post-line."

"Actually that's pretty good," Landsaw said. "Thanks."

Jagger returned to Dickens while Landsaw sought out the art stacks. On the shelf before the Manet, Matisse, and Monet volumes was a retrospective of Lang's work. The slim and highly stylized book cracked crisply when Landsaw opened it. Lang being just around the threshold of fifty, Landsaw thought it pretentious that the recently regarded artist should have such an omnibus in print already. Landsaw passed through its pages, each of them dedicated entirely to a single piece of Lang's bold tones, quartered neatly within dark lines of wavering width. In strange angles bisecting pastures of subdued hues, Lang captured calamitous abstraction in the slightly humorous chaos of arbitrary arrangement. Landsaw could not decide what it was that imbued energy into Lang's pictures, but he could not deny it was there. Blocks of turquoise splashed onto washed-out pinks and hot reds were set upon dead blacks, allowing the saturation of his brush to show with one color, but not the other.

"Rummaging through refuse are we?" a voice asked from behind.

Landsaw turned to discover Lang, and laughed nervously in response.

"They must have just ordered this," Lang said. "Knowing I'd check."

Landsaw closed the book and considered its cover as though just noticing what it was.

"And what do you do?" Lang said.

"I'm a student," Landsaw answered.

"No," Lang said. "I know that. You're a student of mine, aren't you? I mean as an artist. What do you do?"

"Oh," Landsaw said. "Paint. Paintings. I mean I paint paintings. Copies, mostly."

"Copies!" Lang said. "Brilliant. The best way to learn. We'll be doing a bit of that ourselves, later in the term. You'll have a leg up, won't you?"

Landsaw did not know if Lang expected him to answer, but he did anyway and said that he guessed that he would.

"Are you checking that out then?" Lang asked, nodding at his book.

"Just looking," Landsaw said. "I finished my line."

"Wonderful," Lang said. "I was hoping I might borrow it myself. I neglected to bring my own."

Landsaw handed the book to Lang, who leafed through it slowly.

"You know," Lang said. "I remember very little about creating any of these."

Landsaw said nothing as Lang continued to ogle his own work.

"I feel no connection to them whatsoever," he continued. "It is as if a complete stranger painted them. Isn't that bizarre?"

"Isn't that the point?" Landsaw asked.

Lang looked up.

"Isn't what the point?" he asked.

"To capture something that's going to go away if you don't?" Landsaw said. "Capture it? I mean like record it?"

Lang looked at Landsaw.

"That is right," he said. "Very good. I would be very interested to know if you believe that what you do, with your copying, achieves this as well."

"I don't know," Landsaw said. "I haven't thought about it that much."

"Perhaps you will," Lang said.

Lang reopened the book and returned to it.

"You know some of these are quite good," he said.

Landsaw uttered an assent and told Lang that he was going off to find his friend. He expected a "very good then" or the equivalent from Lang, but the artist said nothing, and Landsaw backed away, leaving Lang among the stacks, enraptured by the pictures to which he no longer felt a connection.

NINE

The objective," Lang told his class, "is to endow each line with subliminality. To create something true. An entire universe in every stroke."

The class sat in a circle in the studio and Landsaw could not see if Julie's line was it's own universe or not. Lang said it was. Landsaw's line, which Jagger had drawn, was too. Many other students' lines were not. Lang walked from student to student, drawing his own apparently profound lines beside those that failed to capture the entirety of existence. He cocked his wrist with great affectation as he drew. The others were instructed to write about how they composed their art world lines.

"I found a secluded cliff about the water," Landsaw wrote. "I meditated there for an hour and then walked to the library, repeating to myself the mantra a monk had given to me when I was a child. And then I drew my line."

A student raised her hand to protest the exercise.

"Can we do something harder?" she asked. "This school is really expensive and I'm sorry, but I'm pretty sure I know how to draw a line."

Lang considered this.

"You're right," he said. "University certainly is expensive. But—what is your name?"

"Tina," the student said.

"Tina," Lang said. "Listen to me, Tina, if you will. I have exhibited in some of the world's most significant galleries. I am currently at the tip of the tongue of many significant critics. I have studied with masters of the form, who themselves studied with masters of the form, who themselves studied with progenitors of the modern discipline, do you understand? For one full year I drew nothing but lines. You would like to do something hard. I would gladly give you something hard, Tina, but you would be incapable of appreciating it. And if you believe that mentioning on your C.V. that you studied under me is not a tremendous return on your parents' expense," he continued, "then I invite you to withdraw from this course and find one that better accommodates your obviously advanced abilities."

The class watched Lang.

"Excuse me," he said, and walked out.

In his office with the door closed, Lang unscrewed a plastic fifth of whiskey and filled his mug halfway. The embossed airplane dragged a banner over the Eifel Tower. The banner said 1927. Lang leaned back in his chair and looked out the window. The campus trees were brassy in the sunlight against the sea-blue sky deepening behind them. Lang's rage overwhelmed their appeal, and he churned Tina's offending insolence in his head until a knock at the door stirred him, and he rushed to hide his drink in a drawer. Pond entered and Lang stopped pretending to find something to do.

"Ah," Lang said. "Just you then."

"As you were," Pond said.

He tapped at a glass flask tucked into his jacket pocket and Lang retrieved his cup from the drawer.

"Going well today?" Pond asked.

"Not so well," Lang admitted. "Some of these children are twits. Their ingratitude is disgraceful."

"They come from privilege," Pond agreed, "and virtually no life experience."

He sat on the new green sofa Lang had managed to cajole from the administration and retrieved the booze from his pocket. For a moment they sat without speaking, drinking in the quiet reprieve of Lang's office.

"They gave you a rug, too," Pond noticed.

"Hideous thing," Lang said. "Just drab, like the kids."

"My trick," Pond said, "is to find one or two students with some promise. Single them out and ignore the rest. You'll go mad trying to make Caravaggios out of accountants, you know."

"Sound advice then, Pond," Lang said. "You should be teaching philosophy, perhaps."

Lang took a long pull.

"I would also advise," Pond continued, "that you not give too much of yourself to them. Know what I mean? These kids are animals and we're their trainers. They'll dominate you if you bare any vulnerability at all."

"Ah but that's where we differ," Lang said. "I possess no vulnerabilities."

He smiled at Pond.

"But you're right," Lang said. "I'll keep myself to myself. I don't wish to be ripped apart by the preppy panthers, do I?"

He checked the clock above the door.

"I'd better be back then," he said. "They'll think they've run me off for good."

When Lang returned, half of the students were gone.

"They didn't know if you were coming back," said a student with acne.

39

"Of course I was coming back," Lang said. "I was just grabbing my notes."

He looked to his empty hands, hoping prop papers might manifest suddenly.

"Regardless," he continued, "those who are here are marked present. The ones who left are absent. Class was not dismissed."

He looked around the room, the edges of which were now softened. He studied the students in broken glances, jumping from face to face, wondering which ones among them would become his chosen few. The students stared back with empty discomfort.

"So," Lang said finally. "Lines, yes?"

TEN

Lang, Pond, and Frances watched the lake from the porch as Mingus' *East Coasting* drifted in from the living room through the open window.

"Here is one of the great differences between our countries," Lang said. "The Irish have no jazz. It's just not in us."

Frances licked the edge of a yet-rolled joint and rolled it. A pink sky lingered behind the mountains across the water. Behind the illuminated window of a neighboring house, a woman pulled her dress up over her head before a mirror.

"Well there's some excitement," Pond said, standing. "Who needs a refill?"

"Yes," Lang said. "Thank you."

"I have nothing tomorrow," Frances said.

She curled her legs beneath her on the wicker couch and handed her empty glass to Pond. "Why not?" she said.

Pond's hands full with empty glasses, he opened the spring-shut door with his foot and disappeared inside. Lang and Frances absorbed the quickening dusk, with the lake's silver surface flickering under the dimming light, as though trying to communicate something before going dark.

"Just marvelous," Lang said.

"I don't know if John told you," Frances said, "but you're welcome to invite your students over here if you want. We've done it a couple times. Usually only the smart ones show up, so there's plenty of space. And getting them off-campus and plied with a few drinks, they actually tend to appear as somewhat interesting."

Lang raised his eyebrows.

"And spend even more time with those cretins, who are just now driving me into my third drink before dinner?" he said. "But something to consider perhaps."

"If you do it soon you can swim," Frances added.

"Is the water nice to swim in?" Lang asked.

"Nice enough," Frances said. "And still kind of warm."

"I'll have to get some new trunks then," Lang said.

Two weeks later, Lang was in his new trunks, drunk and prattling as he toured the Ponds' packed living room, sloshing vodka from a rapidly emptying handle into his students' readied cups.

"This should enlighten you plenty," Lang told them. "All you drink is beer. Beer beer beer, night after night. Beer is for boys. Beer is for rednecks."

He twisted down to Julie and clinked the neck of his bottle with the rim of her cup. Her cheeks were crimson and her eyes bright as she improvised a seat from Landsaw's knee.

"So you are a couple then," Lang said. "I was going to suggest you should be if you weren't already. Very good then."

He turned to address the room of sodden students.

"Listen to me," he said. "I am pissing. And after I piss, we are swimming. It is a must. It is a requirement. Like the mighty sperm, if you do not swim, you will fail. Agreed?"

The students glanced at each other to gauge the room's collective enthusiasm.

"We don't have suits," one of them said.

"Wear what you want," Lang said. "It is dark and nobody will see you. And we will be working with live models next week, so perhaps this is a splendid time to become more comfortable in the presence of the human anatomy. Okay then. One minute."

Lang left the living room and Julie turned to Landsaw.

"Are we?" she asked.

"If you want," Landsaw said.

"We can find our own spot," she said. "Probably the last chance of the year."

Soon Lang reappeared, holding an armload of tropically colored beach towels that he tossed to his students.

"To the shore!" he announced.

Out the screen door and down a gravel path, the students wound in varying states of undress to the beach. The sand was coarse and cold, but the water, when they waded to their ankles, was warm. The embers of an abandoned bonfire smoked off in deep red cubes nearby. The stars were out and pale behind a veil of overcast. Julie watched the night as she slid from her clothes, which she folded and stacked upon a rock. Landsaw left his bunched up on the sand. A student who had brought tequila to the party was the first to run into the water, naked and yelling as the black lake splashed to white chop around him. Howls and claps encouraged him from the shore. Lang, in his loud trunks, tiptoed far enough out into the water to execute a shallow dive that was more like a belly flop. Landsaw found Julie's hand in the dark and they waded in slowly to their waists before going under. The rest of the class ensued, and soon a circle of heads formed just past where any of them could stand.

"Did anybody think to bring out something we might drink?" Lang asked.

Landsaw volunteered to swim back and dispense the case of beer that had been spared from the party and carried to the lake.

"If we must," Lang said.

Landsaw swam away and Lang disappeared below the surface. The students gasped small, cold laughs as they looked around to see where their professor might emerge. Julie was spinning in place to stay warm when she was suddenly pulled under. She yelled out, but the lake filling her mouth cut short her cry. Lang surfaced nearby a moment later, laughing and wiping the water from his eyes. Julie emerged coughing soon after.

"You're okay then?" Lang asked.

Julie heaved handfuls of water at Lang.

"I thought you were a monster," she said.

"I am though," Lang said, laughing.

Landsaw called out from the shore and began to lob beer cans toward his classmates and professor. The cans landed with deep kerplunks and bobbed back up. He emptied the case and swam back out.

ELEVEN

Lang was standing in the center of the studio.

"As you know," he said, "your Beaumont Museum has granted me an exhibition, which ceases when my time here does, at the semester's end. For what will become your final project, you will go back there and spend time with a particular picture of mine, the one I called *Humbug*. You will each produce a replica of *Humbug* in your own hand, as close to the original as you can make it. As we will learn in the coming weeks, there is a lot to uncover in retracing an artist's steps. And as *Humbug* is my own, you have unique access to the very artist whose steps you are retracing. Understand?"

Lang looked around the room.

"You find me terribly conceited, don't you?" he asked his class.

Some smiled at the question but nobody said anything.

"Well, please accept this gift, by way of apology for my conceit."

From a leather valise Lang withdrew a cardboard box containing small tubes of green paint.

"This is viridian," he said. "Not the cheap American junk viridian, the Jack Daniels viridian. This is the good stuff. The Johnny Walker Blue viridian. You'll need plenty of it for *Humbug*. Grab one as you leave, yes?"

"He is fucking conceited," Landsaw said to Julie as they walked back from class to Landsaw's apartment. "There's no technique to learn from with this. It's all abstraction. Just lines and colors."

"That's pretty much what all paintings are, right?" Julie said. "Lines and colors?"

"It's sick," Landsaw said. "He just wants us to stroke his strokes. It's masturbatory."

Julie strained her face in mock profundity.

"But if we're the ones doing the stroking..." she said.

Landsaw leaned into Julie, pretending to drive her off the sidewalk and into traffic, but Julie jogged ahead to leave Landsaw flailing as he lost his balance. She ran back to steady him, laughing as they continued down the leaf-padded sidewalk.

Hours later at the Beaumont, a student stationed at the front desk and reading a disintegrating copy of *The Monkey Wrench Gang* neglected to notice Julie and Landsaw walk in with their sketchpads and charcoals.

"Lines and colors," Landsaw said, scouting for *Humbug*. "Fuck this."

"Shut up, Landsaw," Julie said. "Isn't this like what you do? Copy paintings?"

"Yeah but I copy classics. Stuff that might actually inform something original if I ever felt like it. Not bullshit pictures."

They located *Humbug* on the east wall of the back gallery.

"Well I almost like it," Julie said. "So make one for me. Give me pointers."

"That grabby professor will give you a pointer," Landsaw said.

"Get over that," Julie said. "He didn't mean anything."

"Feeling you up underwater?" Landsaw said.

"He did not feel me up, Landsaw," Julie said. "He just grabbed my foot. Very publicly I might add. If he was going to make a move on me I don't think he'd do it in front of our entire class."

"He's coming for you," Landsaw said. "I can tell."

"Not that your jealousy and complaining isn't super attractive," Julie said, "but I think it wouldn't be such a bad thing for you to let this go."

"Who's jealous?" Landsaw said. "Just looking out for you is all I'm doing."

"Well you're doing it shittily," Julie said. "Now stop talking, and draw."

TWELVE

Early snow drifted over the campus in sheets, covering the thin slick of ice that had formed from the preceding rain. Cars careened into one another as the hills surrounding St. Bart's became impassable, though Landsaw and Julie had left before the heavy weather to cross the state line into Vermont. They were visiting Ruth, presently passing acres of unspoiled pasture yet to be developed and named for the fragile ecosystems the inevitable condos would displace. The wind blew so that the light snow appeared to fall from below. Derelict barns leaned like drunks and a farmer crossed the road with his herd. Waiting in the Packard, Landsaw and Julie watched the steam from the animals' breathing rise up into a collective cloud.

Everything in Landsaw's house seemed smaller to him, including Ruth. She walked from room to room with a listlessness he did not recognize, and he considered her edging into a life lived alone in a space she had made for two. The house was clean and organized. She had broiled sausages with peppers and onions to serve over rice and the rooms were filled with the wonderful aromas of her cooking. She tossed a heavily dressed salad and presented a pan of apple crisp to be served over vanilla ice cream for dessert. Julie tried to clear the plates when they were done, but Ruth stopped her and poured more wine.

"Sure you're ready for another winter up here?" Landsaw asked Ruth.

"Of course," she said. "Almanac says it's going to be a light one anyway."

"Ron's plowing?" Landsaw said.

"Always has before," Ruth answered. "Why wouldn't he now?"

"Are you going away anywhere?" Landsaw asked. "Someplace warm?"

Ruth looked to Julie.

"Does he do this to you?" she asked her. "Bring something up without bringing it up?"

Julie let her smile answer Ruth.

"I'm perfectly capable of living by myself, Tom," Ruth said. "Is there something that you've seen tonight to suggests otherwise? Am I babbling incoherently? Did I forget to cook the food?"

"I just want to make sure you're getting out is all," Landsaw said. "There's no one to talk to out here."

"You could call me," Ruth said. "But despite what you may want to believe, you are not the only aspect of my existence, and you most certainly have not been a reliable means of preserving my sanity. Anyway you're hogging the conversation. Go do your laundry or something. I want Julie to talk."

"Don't scare her," Landsaw told Ruth.

He stood up and went into the hallway to retrieve the sack of dirty clothes he had brought with him.

"Oh and I don't want to hear any horseshit about you going all the way back over there tonight," Ruth called to Landsaw. "You're staying here."

"That's up to Julie," Landsaw said. "She might have a class or something."

Julie shook her head.

"No class," Ruth said. "Nice try. You'd be hung up on a guardrail somewhere and buried for days."

Landsaw threw the bag down the basement stairs and followed as it tumbled.

"So," Ruth said to Julie. "Tom told me you share the same dreadful professor. From Scotland or something."

"Ireland," Julie said. "And Landsaw, I mean Tom, thinks he's dreadful. I'm less bothered by him."

"I wonder what about him Tom doesn't like," Ruth said.

"I think it's just his style," Julie said.

"Like he's mean?" Ruth asked.

"Not mean," Julie said. "Just maybe kind of tactless? And he's really direct."

"Oh Tom hates that," Ruth said. "Everything needs to be implied with him, if you haven't already noticed. And he cringes at the slightest bit of conceit. Though it's not like his own modesty is setting any records, you know?"

Julie laughed.

"Irish," Ruth repeated. "Is he good looking?"

"In a way," Julie said.

"How old is he?" Ruth asked.

"I'm no good at that stuff," Julie said. "Not very old. Late forties?"

"A little young for me then," Ruth said.

"Are you looking for a date, Mrs. Landsaw?" Julie asked.

"Always," Ruth said. "Especially since I've apparently entered my doddering spinster years."

Julie laughed again.

"As much as I miss Tom, it is nice to not have him around constantly, if you know what I mean."

Julie said she knew. She lifted her wine glass from its bowl.

"Did Landsaw not like that?" she asked Ruth. "You dating?"

"He would try to be supportive on occasion," Ruth said. "But it's tough. I'd tell him I was going on a work trip or something, when the truth was I was up in town or even just a few roads away. Not that this was a regular occurrence. I don't want you thinking I was sleeping my way through the county like some hillbilly harlot. Just a few companions over the years is all. None of them right though, evidently, and eventually I stopped trying altogether. It was just easier than sneaking around Tom. Isn't that ridiculous? Letting your kid scramble your love life like that? Never mind what Mr. Freud would think. But boy would I feel awful. He can really make you feel bad, you know? I don't mean to scare you or anything, because he is a wonderful person and he really seems great around you. But I better tell you that now. He's sweet just about always, but when he feels slighted or something, you know. You know?"

Ruth stared into the table and Julie watched Ruth's face, waiting for her, when she was ready, to surface.

THIRTEEN

COUNTER REFORMATION. Lang slashed the words on the blackboard and turned to face his class.

"What's this?" he asked.

He watched for any signal of recognition, though only the HVAC hummed in response.

"Nobody?" Lang said. "Okay then. Let us start with this."

He erased *COUNTER* from the board.

"What's this?" he asked again.

Again the class regarded him blankly.

"Let me ask you," he said. "Who is Catholic in here?"

Lang raised his own hand and a few students followed, Tina among them.

"Okay then, Tina," Lang said. "Let us pick on you. What does it mean that you are Catholic?"

"That I believe in God?" Tina tried.

"Sure," Lang said. "Sure you do. But so do Muslims and Jews and Southern Baptists. What is it that sets Catholics apart? Aside from the Eucharist and baptisms and all of that such ceremony."

"Um," Tina said. "We ask God for forgiveness?"

"That's good," Lang said. "Very good. We are getting there. But what else, quite plainly, is not only our belief in salvation or forgiveness, but that our salvation will come to us if we are what?"

Lang waited.

"If we are what, class?"

"Good?" someone offered.

Lang snapped his fingers and pointed at the student.

"Yes," he said. "Good. Good is good. Good is right. We believe that we can achieve salvation if we are good. If we are good, God will love us, right? Now what good means we don't have time for in our remaining minutes. And so what about Protestants? What do they believe in? I'll just tell you to save us some anguish. *Sola fide*. Justification through faith alone."

Lang returned to the blackboard and scribbled *SOLA FIDE*.

"The Protestants believe that we can only know God through faith. Through belief. It doesn't really matter how we act, as long as we believe. Seems a fine distinction, doesn't it? No problem, right? It's salvation either way, just through different means. Are you about to punch the nose of your roommate if he or she thinks they're getting saved through faith when you think goodness alone will save you? Who cares, yes? You will go out for beer and pizza regardless. Well the Protestants cared. Quite a lot in fact. They cared so much that England made adherence to Catholicism an act of treason punishable by...does anybody know?"

Nobody knew.

"Punishable by hanging, drawing, and quartering," Lang said. "And do you know what that is? It's bloody disgusting is what it is. You well enough know what being hanged is. So even before that, they would drag you by horse to the gallows. But they would only hang you so much. You would not die, but you would wish you had. A quick death was far too lenient for the Protestants. Remember these are people who did not care much for piety. You would only almost die on the gallows, but they would take you down before that happened and they would cut off your unit—sparing the women from this business by simply burning them alive—and then disembowel you, cut off your head, mercifully, and then quarter you. Quarters are fourths, are they not?"

With his hand Lang sliced down his torso and then sliced himself sideways.

"And so that is what they would do. After collecting the pieces, they would prop them up publicly to make sure everybody knew how much good being good would do them."

Lang checked his class for signs of squeamishness or disdain.

"Still with me?" he asked. "Okay then. So where are we going. That was the Reformation. And what happened next?"

Lang rewrote *COUNTER* over the faded letters he had erased on the board. The class chanted out the full phrase in unison.

"Very good," he said. "We are learning."

He moved to the center of the circle.

"The Catholics weren't so keen on being chopped up and nailed to a bridge. They wanted to go back to the old days, with their pageantries and relics. They wanted moral reform. Write that down, *moral reform*. Some of you could do with some moral reform indeed, I can tell. Like getting your spiritual oil changed, isn't it? Internal renewal. But how do we get there? Aside from councils and doctrines and treaties and all that dreadfully dull mishmash. How do you spiritually cleanse an individual? An everybody. A simpleton. A dunce. Through what means? What method? This is something all of you should know."

"Through art," Julie said.

54

Lang beamed.

"Through art," he repeated. "The Catholics needed artists. Can you imagine? A society, a religion, a government even, needing artists? These days we artists are outliers. Fanatics; hobbyists; painters of pretty pictures that are nice but are not necessary, yes? But for the Catholics, art was the gospel. The arts meant social integrity. They were necessary. How else would you get through to the morality of an illiterate peasant? Pictures. Images. Subliminality. And it mattered very little how original the art was or who created it. It just had to be effective. And so enter..."

Lang turned back to the board and wrote out *SASSOFERRATO*, pronouncing the syllables in clumps as he wrote them.

"Does anybody know this person? Mr. Thomas? You studied in Italy, correct? Did you encounter the great Giovanni Battista Salvi da Sassoferrato while you were there?"

Landsaw shook his head.

"How about this guy then?" Lang said.

He wrote out *RAPHAEL* and the class murmured in recognition.

"I thought so," Lang said. "Everybody knows him. They even knew him in the 17th century. Maybe not as well regarded as his friend Michelangelo, but regarded nonetheless. And suddenly, with the return of reverence for holy representation, there was a market for him. The only problem with Raphael was that he was dead. And with many of his great religious paintings and those of his contemporaries hidden away, damaged, stolen, or even destroyed, the Catholics needed new ones. And so they raised the dead. Not through resurrection, but through resemblance. This is what Sassoferrato did. He copied Raphael. Not in a deceitful way like the fakists did, smudging their canvasses in ash to age them for profit. Sassoferrato produced honest copies and sold them as such. In turn, he birthed his own style of emulation and imitation, transcending mimicry. His copies served a function, not to deceive, but to renew. Accuracy was not paramount in these copies. But evocation was. The conjuring of the divine that his predecessors had channeled through their hands."

Lang walked to a corner of the studio to retrieve a slide projector strapped to a rolling cart. He walked it back to the center of the room and plugged it in.

"Someone close the lights," he said.

Lang pulled down the vinyl screen coiled above the blackboard and clicked through the slides until a faded Madonna slid into view.

"Okay," he said. "This is Raphael's *Garvagh Madonna*. So named because of Lord and Lady Garvagh, the rich people who owned her before she made her way to London. That's Jesus," Lang said, pointing at the haloed cherub in his mother's lap.

He pointed to the second child in the painting, swathed in an animal pelt and bequeathing a pink dianthus to Christ.

"This one is John the Baptist," he said.

"Beautiful, no? Divine? It is considered almost perfect, save for some awkwardness around the lady's leg over there."

Lang waved his hand to the bottom left edge of the painting before clicking the slide control to the next image.

"This," he said, "is the same painting, effectively, but done by Sassoferrato. Does it matter that the halos are gone and the dress is now blue? Look closely. Even the flower is missing. But do you not get the point? Does it not do its job to evoke its antecedent, with the grace and goodness of the original intact? Now look at this one."

Lang clicked the slide again to Christ's baptism at the Jordan River.

"Here they are again," Lang said. "Christ and John. This time older, with John baptizing the Lord. This one's by Pietro Perugino. And this," Lang clicked again, "is Sassoferrato's copy. Similar, no? Almost exact. Not just in content but in style, too, no?"

Lang clicked the slides back and forth a few times.

"The latter painting is so similar, in fact, that despite Mr. Sassoferrato never intending to confuse anybody's understanding of who painted it, the National Gallery in London made somewhat of a famous bungle of it by first declaring it to be a true Perugino. But then later, the museum decided it was a fake. We now know that neither of those charges is true, and that the truth, as usual, is somewhere in the middle. You must understand that a fake is only declared as such when there has been an intent to deceive. Write that down; *intent to deceive*. When some charlatan tries to sell or present a piece as something it is not, that artwork is a fake. Now one such gentleman did deceive the National Gallery's director into believing this was a genuine Perugino, and once the fraudster was identified, the painting was dismissed along with the schemer and the director's reputation. But it is interesting that nothing about the painting's composition or content changed, isn't it? Only the baggage behind it did. The bullshit. In Sassoferrato's time, all of that mattered much less. What mattered was the meaning. The message. But here in our time, we value authenticity to an exorbitant degree. We care about the artwork as an object and its value as such. What its substance represents is nearly incidental. But just for lack of anything better to do, some scientists took bits of paint from this supposed fake and discovered no modern pigments. In fact, it contained an antimony yellow used exclusively in 17th century Rome. Some smart people got together and realized that while Sassoferrato was busy copying Raphaels at the San Pietro, he most certainly would have seen Perugino's painting, and isn't it likely that he made a copy of that one, too? And so suddenly, the painting became interesting again. It was no longer a fake Perugino, but a genuine Sassoferrato. A genuine copy. Again, nothing about the artwork itself changed, only the story applied to it. But this was enough to invert its value twice over."

Lang looked at his class.

"Have I bored you completely?" he asked. "This is a lot and I am sorry, but I'm almost through. Just one more slide."

He clicked to *Humbug* and the class groaned.

"Already hate this do you?" he asked. "Well I hope you are sick of it. I hope it haunts your dreams the same way Raphael's and Perugino's paintings must have haunted Sassoferrato. But unlike Sassoferrato, who could not ask Raphael how he achieved this technique or ask Perugino the method for blocking out the background, you, my flock, have unfettered access to the artist you are copying. You can ask me how I worked. In fact you must ask me in order to earn an A, do you understand? Remember that I am not looking for exact copies, but you must translate the essence."

Lang turned off the projector and called for the lights to come up. The class shuffled their notebooks into their bags in preparation for dismissal.

"Alright," Lang said. "I have troubled you enough for today."

FOURTEEN

So you're leaving?"

Landsaw swung the Packard around the broad curve past the empty campus playing fields. The first storm had all but melted and the fields held small reservoirs that reflected the fall decay, which had stripped to sticks the trees between the evergreens.

"Just for two nights," he said. "And I told you you should come with us."

Julie looked at Landsaw to see if he believed honestly that she would.

"And watch you and Jagger get drunk and catch, or more likely, not catch fish all weekend? I'm good. But why are you going again? You don't even fish."

"I fish," Landsaw said.

"What kind of fishing pole do you have?" Julie said.

"It has a cork handle," Landsaw said.

"What's the biggest fish you ever caught?"

"I think it was called a brownfish," Landsaw said. "One word."

"See?" Julie said.

"We're getting off campus to enjoy nature before everything disappears under the snow," Landsaw said. "What could be better?"

"Name literally anything," Julie said.

"Nailing your hand to a tree," Landsaw said.

"That actually does sound better," Julie said.

"Eating glass," Landsaw said.

"Dish it up," Julie said.

"Well *bon appétit*," Landsaw said. "We're going to have fun."

"I have that fake to work on anyway," Julie said.

"Copy," Landsaw corrected.

"Copy," Julie said. "It will be good to focus on it without you distracting me."

Landsaw idled the Packard by the entrance to Julie's building.

"And it will be good for you," she said. "You and Jagger can talk about me and whomever he's porking."

"Gross," Landsaw said. "And I'm not sure you fully grasp the concept of this excursion."

"You won't talk about me?" she asked.

"Maybe philosophically," Landsaw said. "Like as a Platonic ideal. But not specifically. And certainly not in the realm of porking."

"Alright Aristotle," Julie said. "I'm sure you'll both come back wiser and spiritually renewed, not hungover and feeling like shit for being dumb all weekend."

"Guess we'll see," Landsaw said.

"Right," Jagger said, lifting a twenty-two to an empty Schlitz can, set on the back of a decoy deer. "That sounds much harder than drawing a line."

He fired the gun, obliterating the can. Buckshot scattered across the lake beyond the decoy, and the echo from the blast broke in sequence like thunder across the surrounding hills. Jagger approached the target with a quarter-full can in-hand.

"Don't shoot yet," he told Landsaw.

He slugged the remaining beer and balanced the empty on the decoy. A loon swooped to a stop on the lake and floated within their range.

"Get the bird out of there first," Landsaw told Jagger.

"Hey," Jagger called to the bird. "Hey you. Scram."

Landsaw loaded the gun and they both watched the loon swim out of the way.

"Okay," Jagger said.

The cabin belonged to Jagger's uncle. He had offered it to Jagger on the condition that he clean the place up ahead of his and his hunting buddies' arrival the following week. When Jagger and Landsaw had arrived, they had mousetraps to empty, outdoor trash cans ripped to ribbons by raccoons to attend to, a coating of dust to wipe away and vacuum up, and mildew to bleach in the bathroom. Otherwise, the cabin was dreamlike in its solitude of possibility. A room-spanning window filled the main lounge with a lakefront view, and the basement offered an exciting surplus of shotguns, liquor, and pornographic magazines.

Landsaw lined up his shot. He centered the can in the bead sight at the barrel's tip and adjusted the butt off of his collarbone to better absorb the kickback. He flicked off the safety and his finger tested the trigger before committing. But as he was about to fire, a fishing skiff puttered into his scope. A man in a bucket hat and camouflage-patterned poncho waved for Landsaw and Jagger's attention.

"What the fuck are you doing?" he yelled to them.

"Shooting," Jagger said. "Cans. Don't worry, they're empty, haha!"

"There are houses over there!" the man yelled.

"This can't shoot that far," Jagger responded to the man. "Fucking renters," he said to Landsaw.

"One more shot and I call the state," the man said.

"Lemme see that," Jagger said to Landsaw.

Landsaw handed Jagger the gun and Jagger turned the safety off and set it down across the makeshift plywood table they had been using. He waved to the man that they would stop and the man raised the throttle of his outboard, turning from their dock to motor back out toward the center of the lake.

"I didn't know you had it in you," Landsaw told Jagger.

"I don't," Jagger said.

He picked up the shotgun and quickly fired out into the wake of the fishing boat.

"Fucking renters," Jagger said again.

"Should we be expecting the police then?" Landsaw asked.

"For gunshots at a hunting camp?" Jagger said. "Even if the staties did come out they'd turn around the second they saw this dude's getup. That's the kind of guy who comes up here for solitude because nobody in the real world can take him seriously."

"You can tell that just from the poncho?" Landsaw asked.

"And the hat," Jagger said.

When the guns were restored to their racks in the basement, Landsaw and Jagger removed themselves to the porch overlooking the calm water. The surface was black and silver and reflected the orange orb of the evening's fading sun. Jagger had purchased a film canister of psychedelic mushrooms off of a dining hall cook. Presently he tweezed out the small, gnarled fungus with his fingers and handed some to Landsaw, who gulped them down accompanied by a long swig of beer. Jagger followed, and within an hour they were laughing inconsolably at the concert being performed by the asylum of loons on the pond. The birds were harmonizing in parts too numinous for the far-gone friends to count. Landsaw nearly slid off of his chair laughing when one of the birds took on a falsetto call a full octave above the others. He and Jagger took turns imitating the fisherman as well.

"What the fuck are you doing?" Landsaw managed through tears. "There's a house over there and a boat over there and a tree over there and a dock over there and I'm staying up over there and some loons are singing their goddam beautiful hearts out right around there," and so on until they were both laughing breathlessly from their stomachs. It was the night they invented their band, The Loons, which would exist in theory alone.

Later in the pitch dark they walked to an overlook Jagger knew but could not find with his fading flashlight. The path became less obvious at each twist. Landsaw complicated the maze by driving off through the woods at a heavy clip with the deep autumn leaves crunching beneath his steps. He lost himself in a tangle of trees and discovered a protruding slab of moss-covered granite. He rested upon it, settling the back of his head carefully onto the small ridges of rock. He closed his eyes and suddenly Julie was with him, a Julie of ephemeral light, a glowing spirit, wandering the woods before him.

"Julie," he said to the apparition.

But the vision flickered out and Landsaw was alone again. He watched the clouds, which looked like wolves, move beyond the moon. He watched the lake through the trees, appearing like a series of thin silver daggers. The branches were arranged against the sky like veins. He wondered how he might find Jagger or the cabin. Eventually he heard laughing, which he was troubled to discover was his own.

"What's up?" Jagger asked.

Landsaw sprang up from the rock.

"What?" he said. "Where did you come from?"

"When?" Jagger asked.

"I mean you're there?" Landsaw said.

"Yeah," Jagger said.

"Wow."

"Why?"

"How long have you been there?" Landsaw asked.

"Since we got here?" Jagger said.

"Oh," Landsaw said. "But didn't I—how long has that been?"

"Like less than five minutes?" Jagger guessed.

Landsaw sat up and nodded as though what his friend said had been of profound importance. He looked around the dark forest, suspicious of the trees.

FIFTEEN

Lang pressed his weight onto the polished café counter, mesmerized by the tattooed arm of the barista as she emptied his beans into the grinder. She flicked on the machine; its grating assault agonized his headache. The night prior, he and the Ponds had planned for nothing more than the usual rounds of cocktails at home, but with the warmer reprieve from the recent snow, they had set out to the last bar in town to still have a jukebox.

"The students don't really know about this one," Pond had told Lang.

They had taken turns selecting songs and Lang recalled dancing with Frances. He hoped his booze-smeared memory was exaggerating how closely he had held her, and that a blackout wasn't blocking the recall of an attempted kiss. But he could envision her pulling away from him, laughing to lighten her discomfort. He had the terrible feeling he owed both Frances and John an apology that he would not give.

The barista slid Lang's coffee to him, spilling some of it over the rim of the paper to-go cup. He had asked for a mug to stay, but Lang took the message for what it was. He thanked her and searched the busy café for a table. Single students claimed entire booths with their pages of homework spread in paper explosions around them. Earnest-looking aesthetes crumpled into themselves, broadcasting their greatest imitations of the singular artist. Julie sat in one of two leather armchairs, separated by a wooden table with a stained glass lamp on it. She directed her focus on a paper bag-bound textbook. A black notebook she had decorated with a bumper sticker—"If It's Not Fun, Why Do It?"—lay on the table beside her. Lang approached her and read the sticker aloud.

"And you believe this?" Lang asked her.

Julie laughed.

"I guess so," she said.

"This homework you're doing," he said. "Is it fun?"

"My degree will probably allow me to have more fun than I might have by not having one," she said to Lang. "So maybe? I don't know."

"Very true," Lang said. "But may the reverse not also be true?"

"What reverse?" Julie said.

"If it's fun, why not do it?"

Julie laughed again.

"Sure," she said.

"May I sit?" Lang asked.

"Sure," she said again.

Julie lay beside Lang as he slept. An open window ushered in the cold and she sat up. She caught the reflection of her body in a standing mirror and studied it. She remembered how her dark hair had unspooled across the white sheet. She remembered Lang's hands. She smiled at herself in the dark and thought it ridiculous to be there, funny even, as though the experience were something that had happened to someone else, a story someone else was telling her, which, Julie supposed, it was. She continued watching the mirror. Lang had been overwrought like she had expected him to be, muttering passion-plagued nonsense, quietly, so as not to wake the Ponds. Julie smiled, remembering his awkwardness, and stifled a laugh. She did not feel tired and she thought of leaving, but the walk back to campus in the middle of the night was daunting, and she lay back down, and soon she was asleep.

SIXTEEN

Jagger was cooking an omelet by way of denying his abject condition. He gathered the ingredients and laid them out in a semicircle around his mixing bowl. He charred a red bell pepper over the propane flame before dicing it up and pouring the whisked egg into the frying pan. Carefully, he selected only the unblemished leaves of spinach from the plastic bag and spaced them out among the chunks of feta. When it was ready, he ate the omelet forcedly, and threw it up within minutes.

Landsaw had been sleeping in a small room off of the kitchen and awoke to the retching. His body registered itself as a dry tangle of organs. In the night he had managed to strip the bed of its sheets and himself of his clothing. He awoke half-swaddled in a pink and yellow beach towel of unknown origin. He checked the bedding clumped in the room's corner for dampness. That the sheets were dry only compounded his confusion. He did not remember falling asleep or preparing for bed. He stared with disdain at a nature scene hanging on the wall of the otherwise blank room. The print was done in velvet and depicted a fawn taking respite by a stream. Landsaw wondered why a hunter would enjoy an image of his prey at peace, and was on his way to a nascent theory when dizziness struck and he had to close his eyes. When he opened them, the stream in the painting was running through the frame.

"Jagger," he called through the wall. "I need to get in there, man."

They spent their Saturday prostrate before a primitive TV, watching a Davy Crockett marathon and game shows. They stomached no solids beyond plain waffles, lightly toasted, as they awaited a reasonable hour to switch from coffee back to beer.

SEVENTEEN

Julie came down the stairs holding her bag and jacket. She negotiated each step so as to provoke the least screeching from the age-warped wood. In the early dark of morning, she had dressed and found her things without waking Lang, whose snores she hoped would cover her exit. She saw the landing illuminated from the kitchen and thought she might retreat to find another route, but the prospect of rendering more noise in Lang's direction kept her going down. She thought she remembered an anteroom she might slip out through.

"You can come down," Frances said from the kitchen. "No judgment here. Just coffee."

Julie accepted the remaining steps and discovered Frances at the kitchen counter. There was no anteroom anyway. Frances was sitting before two stacks of stapled pages, her red pen in-hand. Out the kitchen window, a sunrise was beginning to blossom across the lake.

"Coffee's in the coffeemaker," Frances said, still focused on her work. "Mugs are in the cupboard above it."

Frances looked up at Julie.

"You are young," she said.

"What happened to no judgment?" Julie asked.

"You're right," Frances said. "Though it's not such a terrible judgment to be young, is it?"

Julie filled a mug halfway with coffee.

"Cream or sugar or anything?" Frances asked.

Julie shook her head.

"I guess you look familiar," Frances told Julie.

"From school I think," Julie said. "You're a professor?"

"Comp," Frances said. "But reading through these essays this morning, I'm getting the feeling that I've wasted my career, because these papers are dog shit."

Julie took the empty stool beside Frances.

"What are they about?" Julie asked.

"Here," Frances said. "Be useful."

She handed Julie a new essay along with her red pen.

"You edit that one and I'll make you something for that headache."

"Headache?" Julie said. "Oh, I'm not hungover."

Frances made a face.

"Well let me make you something anyway," she said. "Fresh fruit to start the day."

Frances became engaged at the freezer, extracting various bags from its depths and gathering them on the counter. Julie looked down at the essay.

"They all imitate someone," Frances said. "The boys generally imitate Hemingway if they're readers. Him or Kerouac. The Kerouacs are worse in my opinion. I don't know where the ones who don't read get their tone, but it's really embarrassing. The girls write poems even when I tell them to write prose. You'll see."

"What was the prompt?" Julie asked.

"Regret," Frances said.

"This one's about a family vacation," Julie said.

"A lot of them are. She'll tack on a line about regret at the end. Maybe she regrets leaving something behind. A boy she met or something?"

Julie flipped ahead to the end.

"Oh wow," she said. "Sandals."

"Hopeless," Frances said.

She dropped frozen chunks of banana into a blender and added dashes, scoops, and shakes of various powders from glass jars. She dropped in raspberries, added water, and flipped the blender on. It roared to life, filling the room with a high-speed, whining cacophony. Frances watched the blender work until she looked over and noticed Julie's discomfort at the din. She softened the blender to low, briefly, before turning it off.

"Sorry," she said. "These will just be a little lumpier than usual, if that's alright."

Julie smiled politely and Frances poured the concoction into matching cups. Julie heard classical music playing softly in the background and looked around for a radio.

"You can turn it off," Frances said.

"It's alright," Julie said. "I just didn't notice it before."

"It's hard to notice," Frances said. "I don't know why the morning DJ insists on these vapid playlists. Neville Mariner and his pompous St. Martin-in-the-Fields horns all the fucking time. It's like they're actively trying to turn people off to classical, you know?"

Julie said she knew.

"May I assume you're in the art program?" Frances asked.

Julie nodded.

"Do you paint? What do you do?"

"Watercolors," Julie said. "Not well or anything. Not yet I mean."

"At least there's a yet," Frances said. "If you already thought you were good you might be wasting your time. What kind of things do you paint? Mountains and seascapes or more abstract stuff?"

"Mostly mountains and stuff," Julie admitted. "I mean for now."

"Well I'm glad you're not another abstract painter," Frances said. "We don't need anymore of those if you ask me."

Frances stopped grading and looked at Julie.

"Doesn't it drive you crazy sometimes when you read the artist statements that abstract painters attach to their work? Like all of this philosophical horseshit ascribed to basically just random improvisations? I mean, why pretend? Why not just write 'This series of paintings represents a bunch of splotches of different colors that look nice together' or something like that?"

Julie laughed, but an upstairs floorboard creaked underfoot and she stopped.

"It's probably just John," Frances said. "My husband. But not necessarily."

Julie finished her smoothie, smiled at Frances, and stood up.

"See you around, I guess?" Frances said to Julie.

"It was nice talking with you. Good luck with those," she said, indicating the essays.

She left through the living room where the party had been, out through the screened-in porch and into the established daylight.

EIGHTEEN

On Sunday night, following his return from his weekend with Jagger, Landsaw sat at the Beaumont before *Humbug* and sketched. He missed Julie terribly and had called her twice, but she had not answered either time.

The gallery was quiet and empty but for the guard, another student, who had barely noticed Landsaw when he had walked past her with his equipment.

His work was not fruitful. When Landsaw chose the paintings he copied, his interest was the force that drove the work. Either there would be mystique to trace to its source or a mastery of technique that he would reach to understand. But his connection to *Humbug* was merely resentment, and his attempts to copy it began with a series of false starts. His paper was a splotch of grays marred by erasure.

Meanwhile, in Landsaw's bedroom, Julie sat composing a letter, experiencing the same difficulties of a true beginning. She sat at his desk in the glow of a lamp while a squall outside gained speed, dashing snow that sounded like sand grains against the window. She was attempting to write to Landsaw about her night with Lang, but she could not establish the right voice. One draft was too severe, one too breezy, another quite grave. She had assigned herself the challenge of conveying regret for how Landsaw might feel about it while refusing to regret the event itself. She began a draft that focused on the letter rather than the event, but soon crumpled it up. She began again with a tribute to their love, a word neither had breached out loud, but again dismissed the draft.

For a long while she watched the snow gather outside beneath a streetlight. She wished Landsaw were there to help her think of what to say to him, and so she wrote this down, and she continued writing, expecting with each new line to tear out the sheet and start again. But finally she did not, and when she was finished, she sealed the letter in an envelope before she could read it through and change her mind.

Preferring that Landsaw find it in the morning, so as to avoid the portentousness with which evenings dramatize the ordinary, she pulled on her coat and left the letter in his mailbox. She then walked back to her room through the quiet campus in a quickening snow.

NINETEEN

Maybe it just fluttered away. Ever consider that, detective?"
Sunny sat across from Rudy Mawn in Mawn's upstairs
office at the Boylston Theatre, where Mawn had been the
programming director since before the stolen Housemann episode.
To Sunny, Mawn came across more like a construction foreman than
someone who had time and again scoured the byzantine offshoots of
Broadway to find and stage the next theatrical sensation, but his reputation
at the Boylston was renowned, and during his storied tenure, Mawn had
revived the graying Boston theater scene. His most-often deployed tactics
included presenting controversial programming juxtapositions and
taking critical leaps of career-killing faith as frequently as possible. Theater
directors in other cities often attempted to copy Mawn's formulas, quite
regularly resulting in their immediate dismissal, or, in more than one
instance, the permanent shuttering of the building.

Years of cigarette smoking had perfumed Mawn's office air with a
noisome reek so rank that few visitors ever stayed long, a dividend of the
vice which Mawn welcomed. He was drinking more-cream-colored-than-
brown, room-temperature coffee from a Styrofoam cup with no lid.

He was surprised to see renewed interest in the case. When Sunny had mentioned Seward's name, Mawn said he knew him only as the eccentric paramour of an equally eccentric actor, Glenn Boone, who, Mawn griped, had leveraged the impresario's buzz to launch himself to Hollywood.

"You mentioned Boone was a little over the top," Sunny said. "Seward is a serious art collector. You don't see any connection there, do you?"

Mawn crossed his arms and grunted.

"Course I do," he said. "But like I said, it took a fucking crane to get that thing in here, okay? Takes 10 guys, at least, to lift. You think some silly little actor and his boyfriend just carried it away?"

Mawn shook his head.

"What's the interest in the Seward character all of a sudden anyway?" Mawn asked Sunny.

"There's new evidence," Sunny said. "But I'm not at liberty to discuss it."

"Fucking cops," Mawn said. "I mean no offense, but it's like you try to have a conversation, you know? You gotta tell them everything, they don't gotta tell you shit. It's not how talking works, you know."

"What else do you remember about Glenn Boone?" Sunny asked.

"Let's see," Mawn said.

He drew a hand to his chin to affect thinking.

"Pain in the ass, chronically late, fussy about pay, loathed by the crew, argumentative...there's more but you get the gist. All that aside, he could sell tickets like King fucking Kong."

"And where is he now?" Sunny asked.

Mawn looked at him blankly.

"You serious?" Mawn said.

Sunny aped Mawn's empty stare.

"You don't get to movies much, do you, detective?" Mawn said.

"No," Sunny said.

Mawn moved papers around on his desk to unearth the arts section of the day's *Globe*. He pawed through its pages and folded the newspaper over on an article that he handed to Sunny.

"There you go," he said. "Glenn Boone. The way he talks himself up in here though you'd think he was Orson fucking Welles."

The newspaper article regarded Boone's upcoming film, his first as a director. It was a Tarzan-in-the-city picture for which the producers had bet large on Boone's star power to sell.

"They all go to the movies," Mawn said. "They cut their chops here and then move on, that is until they've made their dough and want to jazz up their image by returning to the *theater*."

Mawn exaggerated the word with Shakespearian gusto.

"But I'm telling you, detective, this guy couldn't figure out something like stealing that statue. Would take connections he simply didn't have."

"And Seward," Sunny said. "Did he ever come to the theater?"

"You kidding me?" Mawn said. "Only every fuckin' night. And day, too, if we had a matinee. Sat right up in front. These guys were nuts for each other, until they weren't."

"And when was that?" Sunny asked.

"Who knows," Mawn said. "Probably when Errol fucking Flynn over here lit out for the territory. I remember hearing about some blowout they had at a restaurant in the North End, though. Screaming, yelling, throwing breadsticks and all that shit. But with something like what these guys had for each other? No way it doesn't end without some kind of head-on collision, you know?"

Sunny said he knew.

"Look, detective," Mawn said. "I don't like being rude, but I've got a director to sober up before curtain."

"Of course," Sunny said.

He stood and went to Mawn's window, which looked out over Boston Common. Sunny traced the park's pathways, scanned its ponds, and found the Public Garden. He considered the hibernating flowers below the frozen earth and summoned the smells of a still-distant spring. Mawn grunted.

"Right," Sunny said.

He thanked Mawn and let himself out via the narrow hallway and a steep set of steps. He came through a door that brought him to the side of the theater's expansive stage, where a crew was arranging a set meant to represent a Victorian living room. Sunny walked up the slope of the auditorium toward the rear doors and exited into the lobby. An arrangement of flowers decorated the pedestal where Henrietta Housemann's *Bottom* once stood, silent in the throes of his most rare vision.

TWENTY

The smashed mailbox lay buried in the bank piled high before Landsaw's apartment. Only the broken red flag and split post were visible, protruding from the snow. The tire tracks and smashed headlight from the station wagon that had skid off the road in the night were long since buried, as was the many days' mail the tenants had neglected to collect, Julie's letter among it.

Lang negotiated the embankment with deliberate steps, having failed to find a clear path through to Landsaw's door. He leveraged the packed and frozen snow for balance, but at the crest of the heap, his front leg sunk through and the rear one followed. He barreled through the mound with no attempt at grace, and with soaking socks he took the stairs. He knocked and waited, and after many moments, Landsaw appeared behind the window.

Lang waved a greeting.

"Thomas!" he said when Landsaw opened the door.

Sleep still swelled in Landsaw's eyes.

"Good morning, Tom," Lang said. "I hope I'm not waking you just now."

Landsaw shrugged. "It's fine. What's up?"

"I was wondering if we could talk about a few things," Lang said.

"Now?" Landsaw asked.

"If now is good," Lang said.

"Like the project?" Landsaw asked.

"Sure, Tom," Lang said. "That can be part of it."

"Did something happen?"

Lang looked down to indicate his snow-wet legs.

"May I come in?" he asked.

A living room had been improvised by couches in the apartment's open downstairs quarters. Stereo wires ran the lengths of walls with no attempt taken to hide them. Lang did not recognize the movies and musicians displayed on the tacked-up posters, though the Van Gogh nightscape and melting clocks of Dalí he did, with significant disdain for their obviousness. Lang loosened his shoelaces in the apartment breezeway and worked off his shoes, kicking out the snow frozen to his socks and pants.

"Sorry about the mess here then," he said to Landsaw.

"I think it's fine," Landsaw said.

"I don't mean to startle you," Lang said. "May we sit?"

Lang indicated the circular wooden table piled with magazines, hats, playing cards, and a broken lamp. He cleared some of the detritus into a pile and sat down.

"You're being super weird," Landsaw said. "Are you drunk? I mean, it's okay if you are."

"It is weird," Land said. "And I'm not drunk."

Landsaw watched Lang quizzically.

"We are artists," Lang began. "Aren't we, Tom?"

"Alright," Landsaw said.

"And to me, Tom," Lang continued, "what that means, is that everything we do is filtered through a certain...sensibility. Is that right?"

"I guess so?" Landsaw said.

"And in our professional, or in your case academic for now, pursuits, certain conventions might be neglected, or even excused, don't you think so?"

"I guess I don't really know what you're talking about," Landsaw said.

One of Landsaw's roommates came down the stairs, oblivious to Landsaw and Lang engaged at the table. He entered the open kitchen and began pulling at drawers and cabinets.

"Listen Tom," Lang said. "I believe I have taken something of yours, alright? That is what I'm talking about and that is what I am trying to tell you, god damn it."

Landsaw watched Lang settle himself down.

"I'm sorry to raise my voice," Lang said. "Not some*thing*, of course, but some*one* is what I meant."

Lang flinched as Landsaw's roommate blasted on a radio. The professor looked to Landsaw to suggest that the noise be turned down. Curiously, Landsaw's face worked into a grin.

"Excuse me," Lang called to the roommate, who had begun preparing breakfast.

The roommate noticed Lang and waved a cursory apology before lowering the volume to a still obtrusive but soft-enough drone.

Lang turned back to Landsaw.

"Do you understand, Tom?" he asked.

"I do," Landsaw said. "I get it. And it's a cool idea, kind of. But also kind of fucked up."

"Now I'm the one who's lost, Tom," Lang said. "What is a cool idea?"

"This," Landsaw said. "Messing with us to try to manipulate everyone into a certain headspace or something. Like you're trying to get us to put some feeling into the copies, right? Are you doing this with everyone? That seems like it would take a lot of research into everyone's lives. But you were pretty convincing. But I also think a lot of kids are going to be super pissed off and not handle it so well. Some seem super fragile. Am I the first?"

Lang shook his head and looked hard at Landsaw.

"Tom," he said.

Landsaw read Lang's face.

"I'm here to say that I am sorry, Tom," Lang said. "What I did, interfering, was wrong. But I am returning her. Do you understand? To you."

Landsaw sat up.

"What was that last part?" Landsaw said.

"Which?" Lang asked.

"About the returning," Landsaw said.

"Tom," Lang said. "We must not blame her."

"We don't," Landsaw said. "But if you're returning her like you said, shouldn't you be giving me a receipt? Or is there like a thirty-day policy or something? When did this happen?"

Landsaw's voice was rising sharply.

"I'll leave now," Lang said.

"When did it happen?"

Lang stood up and worked his feet back into his soaking shoes.

"Please be mature about this, Tom," Lang said, pulling his arms back into his coat. "For her sake. I was direct with you."

"You're a shit," Landsaw said.

Lang opened the door and nodded a solemn goodbye at Landsaw before going back down the stairs. Landsaw stood watching Lang walk away. After a moment he turned back inside and picked up the lamp from the table and threw it through the open door after Lang. The lamp soared over the snow-covered lawn and shattered on the shoveled sidewalk, missing Lang completely.

TWENTY-ONE

His impulse was to drive. He gathered a bag quickly before walking to the snow-buried Packard. He thought about Julie and about Lang. He threw his bag onto the passenger seat and walked back to the apartment, soon reemerging with the sketches, canvases, and paints he would need for Lang's assignment. In his head he saw the sea, and so he drove south skewing east. Slices of snowpack slid from the roof, smashing on the road behind him, as he negotiated the quiet highway. The radio faded out when he cut into Vermont at Port Henry and faded back in to a new station as he wound through the mountains. After many hours he was in New Hampshire, feeling his way up the coast.

He guessed at an off-ramp and was soon riding through the seaside strip of a boarded-up beach town, passing shuttered ice cream stands and crab shacks. Closed signs hung askew in the windows of weathered boutiques. On the beach, the gray-green sea climbed the sand. Nearby restaurants and clapboard motels with ocean views sat waiting for no one. Landsaw pulled into the parking lot of a long, two-story motel called the Surfside. The lot was empty but for a minivan parked in front.

The woman at the front desk introduced herself as Ada. She wore a floral blouse and thick glasses and spoke through a regional accent that allowed Landsaw to feel he was somewhere farther away than he was. She regarded him with less suspicion than he felt he deserved. Ada gave Landsaw the keys to a corner room on the second floor that faced the beach. Out the window, Landsaw watched a metal detectorist scan the sand. The winter wind inspired tall waves from the sea, and Landsaw could not evict Julie from his thinking.

He cleared a small desk and moved it to the windows, where he propped a canvas and laid out his sketches for *Humbug*. He balanced an image of Lang's original against the wall and set to work, consulting the sketches and mixed colors with the same orchestrations as his referent, as close as he could render. For hours he heard nothing beneath his brush-strokes but the heater in his room, and by early evening he was finished. He went downstairs in search of food.

Ada was standing behind the long bar off of the lobby, talking to a large man in a flannel shirt. The dark lounge with its decorative nets and buoys held the essence of a ship. There was a stone fireplace with no fire in it and whaling scenes on the wall.

"You must be the fella," said the big man at the bar.

He shifted on his seat to extend his hand to Landsaw, who moved quickly to meet it.

"Welcome to the Surfside!"

"Great place," Landsaw said.

"Wanna buy it?" the man asked, erupting into a phlegmy cackle.

"Ignore Hal," Ada said. "We own it together and I'm certainly not selling."

"For now we do!" Hal said, renewing his worrisome laughter.

"How you doing up there?" Ada said. "Got everything you need?"

"It's real nice," Landsaw said. "I just came down to see if there's a place I might get some food."

Ada's face contracted with concern.

"Well," she said, "this time of year can be tough. Annie's might still be open. Let me give them a call, okay?"

Landsaw said it was okay.

"Ain't we got something here?" Hal said. "No need to send the kid out into no man's land in the middle of the night."

"There's tuna salad from yesterday," Ada said. "But you might want something nicer."

"Hell," Hal said, "sit down and let Ada make you an open face. We'll even pour you a beer. He looks old enough."

"Sounds great," Landsaw said.

He mounted the stool beside Hal and thanked them.

"Ada says you're writing a paper or something up there," Hal said.

"Painting," Landsaw said. "For a class."

Ada served Landsaw his beer and disappeared behind a set of swinging doors behind the bar. The beer was stale from sitting in the keg off-season, but it still tasted good to Landsaw.

"Painting the ocean or something?" Hal asked.

"Actually I have to paint another painting," Landsaw said.

"Paint another painting," Hal said. "How about that. Well we love art, Ada and I. Whenever we get down to the city we like to get to as many museums as we can."

Ada returned and set silverware and a paper napkin out for Landsaw.

"I like the one with the Eskimos and the Indians," Ada said. "Making fires behind glass and feeding their babies and whatnot. Makes you think, my gosh, what it was like back then with basically nothing but a thin little teepee to stop the wolves and whatnot from getting at you!"

"That's the history museum," Hal said. "This man is going to think we're philistines, Ada."

Ada dismissed Hal with a wave.

"Hal I can't reach the bread," she said. "You always put it up so high."

Hal turned off of his stool with a caricature groan and left Ada and Landsaw in the calm of the empty lounge. Landsaw could hear the sea outside and thought he might go to the beach after he ate.

"Another one I like is that one with the missing Botticelli," Ada said to Landsaw. "You been there?"

Landsaw said he did not think he had been.

"The one that was robbed," she said. "A bunch of years ago. They did it in broad daylight while the museum was open and everything. They still got the empty frame hanging there. I suppose they're hoping whoever took it waltzes back in and returns it some day. Doesn't seem too likely though, does it."

"How'd they do it?" Landsaw asked.

Hal returned from the kitchen.

"Do what now?" he said.

"Ada was telling me about a Botticelli someone stole in the middle of the day."

"Oh that's a good one," Hal said. "The thieves dressed up like maintenance people and I guess they figured folks would think they were just cleaning it or something. They're always interviewing the guards whenever there's an anniversary or a break in the case or something," Hal told Landsaw. "But they still haven't caught 'em."

Ada turned back through the swinging doors and Hal, reaching behind the bar, poured himself another beer. He returned to his seat beside Landsaw.

"Hundred million bucks or something like that," Hal told Landsaw. "More money than God. It must be something, sitting with all that money right there and not being able to touch it, huh?"

"What do you mean?" Landsaw said.

"Well they sure as shit can't sell it, can they?" Hal said. "I mean it's one of the most famous missing paintings in the world. Who would touch it?"

"Didn't they think of that before they took it?" Landsaw asked.

"Beats me," Hal said. "Coulda been for other reasons, I suppose, but I can't imagine what those might be."

Ada returned with Landsaw's sandwich and set it down before them. Landsaw thanked her and dug in.

"You tell me how that is," Ada said. "And I bet those criminals found some way to spend that money. Probably living it up in Monaco or St. John's or somewhere. That's what I'd be doing."

Landsaw nodded at the prospect.

"Now what I would do," Hal said and cleared his throat. "And hear this. This is good. What I would do—if I could do it—is I would find some feller who can paint real good, right? Like real good. And then I'd have this guy draw up a Monet or Van Gogh or something like that. Kind of like what you're doing up there, painting another painting. Well I'd have him make his painting pretty close to how Mr. Monet or Mr. Van Gogh had done it, but not too close, okay? Not exact. Something's different. Maybe one of the colors is a little off or the robes ain't creasing right. Something. You following me?"

Landsaw nodded as he chewed and Ada watched Hal with rapture.

"And then," Hal continued, "you have that feller draw it up again! Only this time, he does it perfect. Just like the original. I mean they are the exact same damn thing, okay?"

"Okay," Landsaw said.

"And then what you do is you quietly steal the real painting, but you replace it with the not-so-good copy. Got me?"

"Sort of," Landsaw said. "But why bother replacing it at all?"

"And why the not-so-good one, Hal?" Ada asked. "You have a perfectly good copy already. They would know immediately, with all kinds of experts and art snobs running around the museum all the time. Why not replace it with the real good one?"

"I'll tell you why," Hal said. "Replacing it gives you time to square away the sale. And then you got the real painting *and* the real good copy of it. As Ada pointed out, people are gonna notice real quick that the thing's been switched and that the Monet ain't a Monet. And so people start asking questions, 'My God, where did it go?' or 'How did this happen?' and whatnot. And so what happens?"

Hal raised his right index finger above his head slowly and whistled like a bottle rocket going off.

"The price of this thing soars," he said. "Up and up and up to the goddamn moon. The thing's already one of the most famous paintings out there, one of the most expensive things in the world. But suddenly it's worth double. Triple. Quadruple and so on. 'No questions asked' they would say. 'Anonymous return' or something. 'A billion million dollars or whatever just for a clue.' So you give 'em their clue. Hell you give 'em more than their clue, you give 'em, what appears to be, for all intents and purposes, the damn painting! But do you give 'em the real art? God no. You've got a perfectly good fake right there that could dupe any expert with a magnifying glass. Why not give 'em that one and keep the real one for yourself? That way you have the billion million dollars and the original work of art! How about that?"

Hal had worked himself up and was swatting the table for emphasis. Ada clapped at his plan.

"My husband the art thief," she said. "Go on out there and get us those paintings and the money, Hal!"

"I tell you," Hal said "Someday I might."

"What would you do with the real one?" Landsaw asked.

"Well, keep it I guess," Hal said. "And hell if they ever catch on that the real good fake ain't really all that good, or if they catch on to who did it somehow, well there's your get-out-of-jail-free card right there."

"Brilliant Hal," Ada said.

"It's a lot to think about," Landsaw said.

Hal returned to his beer and took a deep draw to finish it. Then he reached for Landsaw's empty glass and slid it, along with his, to Ada.

"If you would, dear," he said to her.

Ada refilled the glasses and Landsaw returned to his sandwich, devouring it quickly. He spent another hour and another beer with the accommodating innkeepers.

When he returned to his room, he set the heat to high and considered his fresh copy of *Humbug*. It was good, but not exact. Without allowing himself to think about it, Landsaw took the second canvas he had brought and placed it on the desk. Again he consulted the image of *Humbug* hanging there. He dabbed new paint on his pallet, mixing the oils like he had mixed them before, this time taking more care to hold the mixtures to the image, matching them precisely. His first strokes on the new canvas were tentative, but soon he was working out Lang's abstractions with eerie exactitude.

TWENTY-TWO

Had the final Sunday of the fall semester been a regular Sunday, the majority of St. Bart's students would have been pursuing their end-of-week rituals: marathon bouts of homework; escapism into or from the football game; feeding bags of laundry into the basement washers. But this Sunday being one of revelry in the wake of finished finals, the game was observed with fleeting interest only, and the laundry sat unwashed, waiting to be heaved home. Music thrummed from windows propped open by stereo speakers and a medley of cigarette and pot smoke hung heavy in the dormitory hallways. A drunken congregation of hundreds stood amassed outside despite the cold. Nearly every door to every room was left open to invite in the unsanctioned, campus-wide jubilation. But Julie's door was closed. Her roommate had left early for Nyack and the room was hers alone. As she packed she played borrowed cassettes, weaving an invisible mandala in her wake as she moved from dresser to closet to bed and back. At first she assumed the knocking to be another of her roommate's subpar paramours, and she ignored it. When it continued she yelled out above the music.

"She's not here!"

"Yes she is!" Landsaw's voice responded.

Julie opened the door on Landsaw holding a jug of wine and a single drugstore rose.

"There you are," she said.

"There you are," he said.

"I'm sorry," Landsaw said. "I left and didn't tell you. I wanted to finish the copy where I could focus."

"Where was that?" Julie asked.

"The beach," he said. "Turns out it's a lot nicer in the winter. Nobody's there."

"What beach?" Julie said.

"I don't remember what it was called," he said. "It was just a beach, in New Hampshire. Can I come in?"

Julie let Landsaw in and closed the door. He handed her the rose and sat on her bed to unscrew the wine. Julie indicated a stack of Dixie cups.

"It's all we have," she said.

Landsaw poured each of them a full cup, so that the wine formed a slight meniscus at the rims. He tasted it.

"Terrible," he said. "I accidentally left it near my heater so it's kind of hot. I was hoping it would cool down on the walk over."

"Can you stop?" Julie said.

Landsaw looked at her.

"Stop?" he said.

"That's what you do?" she said. "Go to some beach and disappear? I asked you to call me."

"Call you?" Landsaw said. "When?"

"In the letter," she said.

"What letter?" Landsaw said.

"My letter."

Landsaw's face was blank. Julie's drained, too.

"You didn't get it?" she said. "Don't you ever check your mail?"

"Not really," he said. "And anyway someone plowed into the mailbox in the storm the other night. It got all fucked up. You wrote me a letter?"

Julie's expression showed her dismay at having to improvise what she had set down carefully in writing.

"You didn't need to write something," Landsaw said. "That's so formal. You could have just told me."

She looked at him.

"Told you what?" she said.

"About Professor Lang?" Landsaw said. "And what happened, I guess?"

Red now rushed the vacancy of color in Julie's face.

"I'm so confused," she said.

"He told me," Landsaw said. "The other day. He came to my apartment, sat me down, and told me."

"What did he tell you?" she asked.

"Basically that he stalked you down, though those are technically my words, not his."

"That's not what happened," Julie said. "I wanted to write it down so you would understand."

"Guess I missed a real good letter, then," he said.

He stood up and went to Julie's window to watch the crowd that had gathered in the quad outside, all snowballs and yelling.

"The good news," Landsaw said, "and these words are his, is that he is *returning* you to me. Isn't that nice? How does it feel to be returned?"

"He said that?" she said.

"Something like that," Landsaw said.

"Well still," she said, her voice roughened. "I welcomed it, okay? At the time. You need to get that."

"So you wouldn't describe what happened as the result of a basic lapse of judgment?"

"Not really," she said.

"So would you describe yourself as regretful?" Landsaw asked.

Julie sat on her bed with a pillow in her lap and said nothing.

"Guess that's the answer," Landsaw said.

"You need to understand, Landsaw," Julie said.

Landsaw drank the remainder of his cup in one gulp and picked up the jug from Julie's desk.

"Mind if I take this?" he asked.

"Landsaw, sit down," Julie said.

"Have a good flight home and all that," Landsaw said.

He left and Julie yelled after him. The cassette player had the mood all wrong, and Julie poured her wine over it until the music lurched to silence.

TWENTY-THREE

Landsaw parked the Packard as far from the lights as he could and carried inside a copy covered by a sheet. His wet shoes shrieked against the otherwise silent hallways. At the registration desk, a classmate, whom Julie had teased Landsaw about after tracing the track of his eye toward her during a particularly trite Eucharist from Lang, sat reading *Orlando*.

"Hey, it's Tom, from class," she said.

Landsaw couldn't remember if her name was Diane or Diana. He was distracted by her unlikely English accent.

"Hey, it's D," he responded. "From class. Just putting the finishing touches on my copy here."

"Oh, is that it under there?" D asked.

"Yup," Landsaw said. "I just need one more look at the real deal before I'm done."

"Brilliant," D said. "So committed. I'm sure it's amazing. I put literally zero effort into mine. Honestly it took me maybe half an hour."

"Yeah," Landsaw said. "So far me, too, really. Sort of hoping for a Hail Mary with this."

He pretended to look for something that wasn't in his hands.

"Be right back," he said. "Can I leave this here? I left my brushes in the car."

"Right on," D said. "I'll protect it."

As he balanced the canvas against the desk, Landsaw did his best to ignore D's glance, which further confused his already bizarre blend of emotions. He was preparing to steal a painting and had no vacancy for desire.

Landsaw dusted a thin coat of snow from the broad glass pane of the Packard's trunk. He retrieved the small toolbox he had taken from his apartment. Cars glided by slowly under the streetlights on the main road. Back inside, D was gone from the desk but she had left a note beside her upturned paperback: "We close in 20. Drive me home?" She had stylized the zero in the 20 with a smiley face sticking out its foliated tongue.

Landsaw entered the quiet gallery and looked around. As he approached *Humbug*, he allowed that Lang's work now held at least the suggestion of intrigue for him, however complicated. Landsaw listened for a moment before setting to work. He walked up to the wall and put his hands on *Humbug's* sides. He felt the frame and lifted it gently. His palms were sweating. The work felt heavy, something he could manage.

TWENTY-FOUR

Lang's office was in boxes but for the double rows of *Humbug* copies, leaning against two walls, which Landsaw considered from the open door. His own canvas was balanced beside him beneath a black plastic bag. Lang sat with his back to the door, discarding the contents of files into a trashcan.

"What are you going to do with all of them?" Landsaw asked Lang.

"Oh," Lang said.

He turned around to face the door.

"Tom. There you are. I don't know yet."

Lang's Dewar's stood on the desk with no glass beside it.

"I can't take them with me, unfortunately," he said. "Though I would very much like to. Perhaps I can ship a few if it's not too expensive. And perhaps the school will display the rest."

"I can't imagine there's wall space for thirty copies of the same painting," Landsaw said.

Lang laughed slightly.

"I suppose that's true then," he said. "Though some of them could hardly be considered copies, don't you think?"

Landsaw brought in his covered canvas and set it among the others. He looked at his peers' work more closely, pulling some forward to inspect those leaning behind.

"Oh yeah," he said. "Wow."

He looked at Lang and thought Lang looked relieved.

"Well," Lang said. "Of course I've been anticipating yours most of all. Can we see it then?"

Landsaw pulled the bag off of the painting and watched Lang's eyes scan the surface. The rest of his face was still.

"Tom," Lang said after a moment. "What is this?"

"The copy," Landsaw said. "My copy. Of your painting? I mean picture?"

Lang continued to watch the *Humbug*.

"Are you very sure then, Tom?" Lang asked.

"What else would it be?" he said.

Lang was quiet again for a long time.

"It looks," he said finally, "very much like mine."

"Wasn't that the point?" Landsaw asked.

Lang broke his communion with the canvas suddenly and turned to Landsaw.

"Yes," he said smiling. "Of course it was."

"Do I get an A then?" Landsaw asked.

"Of course," Lang said. "A for astounding. I'd like to keep this one with me, Tom."

"Of course," Landsaw said. "It's yours."

Lang began to utter but stopped.

TWENTY-FIVE

Sunny's phone rang. His director at the museum, Raines Halloway, was already speaking when Sunny answered. Sunny grabbed a pen and scribbled.

"L. Placid," he repeated and wrote. "Beaumont. Lorcan Lang. *Humbug*. Yesterday."

The Seward case had occupied inordinate space among Sunny's thinking, but he had kept Halloway in the dark. Halloway had been a ceramicist of modest renown prior to pinballing his way to the highest echelon of fine arts administration. He was nationally renowned, publicly for his discernment and privately for his quiet temper, which could petrify. Sunny knew he should have mentioned Seward to Halloway immediately. That he had not meant it was too late.

"I can be there in a week," Sunny told his boss.

The silence on Halloway's end told Sunny that a week would be unacceptable.

"Five days," he said. "I'm on it."

Holloway's silence persisted.

"I mean three," Sunny said. "I'll leave Friday."

"You leave today, Shimura," Halloway told him calmly.

Sunny tried to think of protestations, but none came to mind.

"The museum is affiliated with the college," Halloway told him. "A dear friend happens to chair the board up there. Let's not provoke him, please."

"No sir," Sunny said. "Just one thing."

"What, Shimura?"

"How big is this lake?" Sunny asked. "Are there waves?"

"It's frozen, Shimura," Halloway said. "Leave the board at home."

The line clicked closed. Sunny left his office for his apartment and began to pack. He took the credit card provided by the MFA but did not take the gun provided by the bureau. He loaded his things into the Mercedes' back seat, started it, and cranked the heat to high. He fled the city along Quincy Shore Drive and over the Neponset River before meeting 93 in Dorchester. On the radio he listened to an interview with a sitcom actor who was bitter over his serial typecasting.

Snowplows idled on-guard between the interstate lanes, awaiting an imminent storm. Sunny encountered only a light flurry as he arrived in New York and pulled into the empty Beaumont parking lot. He had instructions to meet a curator, but the only tracks in the snow were his own. The building's lights were off. Eventually a pickup turned in and took a space beside Sunny. In the darkening twilight, a large man stepped out of the truck and shuffled to the entrance. He unlocked the double doors and flicked on the outdoor sconce, casting new angles of sharp white across the empty black spaces. A moment later, a third car pulled in and parked on the far side of Sunny. A long, heavy jacket with two boots at the bottom got out and traced the larger footprints to the door. In his rearview, Sunny checked his face for the desired affect of severity and killed the engine.

The heavy man was Lance Scheck, head of both Beaumont and Saint Bartholomew's facilities and maintenance. The boots and jacket were Eileen Spitzer, the gallery director. Spitzer removed her coat and halved in size. Sunny noted errant grays among her otherwise auburn curls, which she shook the snowflakes from.

"I understand the artist recently returned to Ireland," Sunny said. "Is that right?"

"Maybe," Scheck said. "I didn't know him. Just knew he was a drinker. Breath like a gas leak, that guy. Sloshed all day."

"Understood," Sunny said. "Did you have a similar impression of him, Ms. Spitzer?"

"He always seemed more hungover than drunk to me," Spitzer said. "But yes."

"His eyes were like two pissholes in a snowbank," Scheck added.

"And what interactions did you have with him?" Sunny asked Scheck.

"Not too many," Scheck said. "Just seen him around. He lived with the other guy and his wife."

"The other guy?" Sunny asked.

"The other professor," Scheck said.

"John Pond," Spitzer clarified. "And his wife, Frances. Both of them are tenured here. They hosted Lorcan."

Sunny wrote this down.

"The Lang exhibition," he said. "It's still up?"

Spitzer led Sunny and Scheck through the lobby and down the hallway to the museum's permanent collection of ancient artifacts, among which were grass masks and wooden utensils, shiny with the signature patina of relics. Scheck followed, his focus reserved for the overhead sprinklers and heating vents. When they entered the main gallery, Sunny's first impression of Lang's art was that it looked dull against the flat gray gallery walls. The *Humbug* in question was isolated on its own panel of wall space. Sunny gazed at it from fifteen feet and then ten before stepping up close enough to unnerve Spitzer, who had trained her docents that that close was too close.

"You hung these yourself?" Sunny asked her.

"Interns helped," she said. "But I hung this one."

"And does anything look different?" he asked.

"Other than the painting itself, not really," she said.

"Where can we look at this more closely?" Sunny asked.

Spitzer set her eyes on Sunny's.

"More closely?" she asked.

"A lab, I mean," Sunny said. "We'll need to check the brushwork of course. And I'd like to look into any craquelure, though with the painting being relatively recent I'm not sure how much we'll find. But a decent light raker should be able to let us at least check it against an image. Though I might start with the pentimenti and X-ray diffraction first. What do you think?"

Spitzer looked offended.

"This museum is very modest," Spitzer told Sunny. "We don't have those capabilities. This is about as close of a look as we're going to get."

"No lab," Sunny said.

"No lab," Spitzer affirmed.

"There's the science lab at the school," Scheck offered. "All sorts of gizmos. Not sure if they have any of what you just said, but I can get you in there tomorrow."

"Will the morning work?" Sunny asked.

"I'm up at three," Scheck said.

"Perhaps nine," Sunny said. "Can you meet us there with the painting, Ms. Spitzer?"

Spitzer agreed and Sunny thanked them both. He and Spitzer walked back through the dark museum while Scheck stayed behind to ensure that anything that had been open was closed and that anything that had been turned on was turned off.

Sunny drove the mostly plowed roads to his motel, passing pubs and pizza parlors lit to fluorescent splendor, a derelict hospital halted under construction, and the slate roofs of battered Victorians, retrofitted into student housing, now sagging under the weight of December snow. Sunny's motel welcomed him with a neon beacon of pinks and blues. The inside was commensurately garish, though the lingering acidity of ammonia at least assured him of an attempt toward cleanliness. The night clerk stood at the desk with a comic book pinned between her hands. Sunny waited as she finished her page. Behind her, a small black and white television set was showing a TV movie.

"Eased up out there," she said eventually.

Sunny hummed his response.

"Just a few nights or you looking long-term?" she asked.

"I have a reservation," Sunny said. "Shimura."

"Oh you," she said, lowering her voice into a raspy whisper. "Eff bee eye. Guess I better be on my best behavior. You know my husband was in law enforcement for seventeen years."

Sunny smiled as politely as his six-hour drive would allow. The clerk flipped through a leather-bound ledger book while Sunny watched the movie behind her. A general was cramped in a bunker with his soldiers, rallying the men to continue fighting.

"We ain't backin' down," the general said. "Not on Christmas."

The camera cropped in closely to the general's soiled face and the clerk turned to watch. Had the soldiers' resulting cheers not given way to a coffee commercial, Sunny was unaware what the glut of his impatience might have inspired. Likely nothing, he admitted.

The queen bed was swathed tightly in sheets and a bandage-colored bedspread folded halfway up toward the hard single pillow. The neon from out front leaked in between the drapes too heavy for their runners.

Sunny dropped his things onto a luggage rack and ran a hot shower. Steam swelled around him as he wrestled the soap from its impossible plastic wrapper. He washed out the long drive and allowed his thoughts to run with the water down the drain. A knock at the door launched him back into awareness. He left the shower running as he stepped out slowly and plucked a towel from the rack. He tiptoed to the door and found that the peephole was clear, though at his feet laid an envelope he deduced had been flicked through the undercut. Sunny opened the door and looked out into the hallway, which was empty. He picked up the envelope and discovered his name upon it, hand-rendered in an elegant script.

TWENTY-SIX

Julie walked the long Upper West Side blocks of broad sidewalks, headed to the park. It had been her father's idea to escape Montana for Christmas, though like many of his impulses, the decision was soon considered through collective regret. The city had seemed exciting until the seasonal sights were seen and indelible tastes tasted, and the Whites found themselves cramped into a fourth-floor walkup, watching television and pining for the capacious solitude they had senselessly abandoned. Julie had been the most disappointed, missing her graceful mountains and their dual promise of solace and danger, whereas the city offered only danger and distraction. She had not wanted to take the train to still more trains and haul her suitcase up the subway steps to a frigid island of sun-blocking monoliths when what she needed was open sky. She had thought of New York as a tireless place where tireless people did tireless things, but not knowing such people, or where such things occurred or how to access them, she wondered what someone like her was supposed to do. She had friends from school scattered about the boroughs and in Long Island, but she did not feel up for the boost in social spirit that such reunions would require. She settled on finding an exhibition or a concert and bought a magazine with local listings. She also bought a pack of cigarettes, though she did not smoke.

At a café on Columbus Avenue the coffee was dark like rich compost and came in a bowl. Julie scanned the listings. Vermeers were in town and a keyboard ensemble was performing a Stockhausen opera at a shipyard on the East River. There was ballet at the Brooklyn Academy and a play with a sitcom actor she liked. As she flipped through the pages, her eyes landed upon a quarter-page ad in a lower-right-hand corner, calling for applications to a women-only residency at a ranch in the California desert. Visions of sagebrush and sunburnt vistas suddenly flashed electric against the dreary urban bluster outside the café. She launched into reverie, considering how her inspiration might thrive in a communal setting, though she also allowed for the likelihood that such an endeavor could prove an expensive gimmick for rich girls who wanted to go west and play O'Keeffe. She decided she would not care if that were true.

On the café's payphone near the single restroom stall in the back, Julie learned that the residency director's name was Katy Karloff, and she had to wonder if Katy's being in New York for the week was not one of those strange miracles that she did not believe in, but which happened nonetheless. They arranged to meet the following day at the same café. Katy was layered in scarves and a woven tunic of obvious expense, embellishing her appeal with earrings of turquoise set in brushed nickel.

"I hate Christmas," Katy said.

She spread sugar evenly from the sides of her spoon over the foam of a massive cappuccino.

"And New York makes my skin feel sick."

Julie sipped at the sambuca she had ordered and regretted immediately, embarrassed by her improvised attempt to signal maturity.

"Also the city has finally killed any last hope of being able to cultivate artists. Do you know what I mean? Like we're lucky this place is still here. Most of these old bars and cafés have become smoothie shops and banks."

"Why are you here if you hate it?" she asked Katy.

"Ex's parents don't know they're ex yet," Katy said. "Part of the deal with me getting the ranch, just to keep up appearances until he figures out how to tell them he's had a change of heart, lifestyle-wise, if you get that. They're very old fashioned and will probably die before he tells them."

"I get it," Julie said.

"I caught him fucking our pot dealer in the outdoor shower," she said. "And I'm not sure 'caught' is the right word. They were probably audible for miles. Sound travels far in empty spaces, you know? Think he was just looking for a way to tell me, and that's the best he could come up with. But anyway, let's talk about getting you out there. What is it you do and when are you looking to do it?"

Julie feigned confidence in telling Katy that she painted watercolors. She knew the stigma of kindergarten classrooms and backwards button-ups for smocks did not represent the tonal infinities that she saw inherent in the medium. She had no pretense that others would readily grasp her private appreciation for the form, though Katy, Julie thought, seemed like she did.

"Do you have a project or something in mind?" Katy asked. "Some end goal?"

Julie felt burdened to invent a thesis.

"The reason I ask is I've found that out there, if you have something specific you want to do before you get there, you have all the time and space to do it. But if you don't, you follow paths that aren't really yours, you know? You start painting the desert or the outbuildings or the people around you, and if we're being honest, there's enough of that shit out there already."

"I don't," Julie admitted. "But I get that, and I will."

"What about school?" Katy asked. "Didn't you say on the phone that you're a student somewhere upstate?"

"I'd go back if I still felt like it," Julie said. "But right now I don't think I do."

"I should tell you that it isn't inexpensive," Katy said.

"I'm thinking I could maybe use tuition toward it," Julie said. "I might ask the college to consider it a semester abroad or field learning or something like that. It would take some persuasion, but I think I can square it."

"Sounds sort of reasonable," Katy said. "And there's nobody here you'd miss? I'd hate to get you out there only for you to find out you want to come home. In other words, no refunds."

Julie was less struck by any concern for missing Landsaw than she was by the realization that she had not thought of him at all.

"It's not a problem," she said. "And it won't be."

"Maybe talk it through first," Katy said. "Because what I won't do out there is mother you."

After a week of Julie's steady prodding, her parents acquiesced. Her selling point had been the mediocrity their money had been buying at St. Bart's, supported with more supplemental evidence than Julie had known she could provide. The only remaining difficulty was to decide whether she owed it to Landsaw to tell him. She thought it odd that someone whose life had run concentric to hers had been so abruptly removed, though her attempts to pity him proved inadequate. At the apartment, watching her reflection against the city behind glass, the best she could muster for him was an apprehension just shy of contempt.

TWENTY-SEVEN

Sunny waited nearly an hour before opening the envelope. He had toweled off, dressed for bed, and read most of the latest *Surfer*, finding particular interest in the public identification of a swell he knew south of Half Moon Bay, which many had thought sacred, permanently reserved for those who had suffered for its discovery.

It was an invitation to a Christmas party. Again he opened the door to his room and checked the hall to see if other envelopes had been slid beneath other doors. None were there, and Sunny called the front desk.

"Nobody I saw who isn't staying here came through," the clerk said.

Sunny could hear the TV behind her.

"And even then," she continued, "aside from you it's only Mr. Lavoie. Been living here five years now. Wouldn't think he's having a Christmas party, but if he is, he's gonna have to clear it with the owners, and I'm not sure that's something they would be up for. Last time someone had a party here the pool had to be emptied afterwards and naked people were hoppin' in and outta taxi cabs all night. Caught one of 'em peeing in my mop bucket! Mr. Lavoie wasn't here then but—"

"Okay, that's fine," Sunny interrupted. "Thank you. Enjoy your movie."

"Oh you bet," the clerk said. "Though I'm kind of losing the plot. Santa Claus is up in space giving presents to the Martian children. I think it's about how he's nice to everyone no matter what."

"That sounds right," Sunny said. "Goodnight."

Sunny re-read the invitation, which said to bring a gift, and a guest.

"That's up on the lake," Eileen Spitzer told Sunny through his motel telephone the following morning.

Cars were sloshing by outside his window in an enduring parade, each of them launching a brackish slop of snowmelt onto the occasional passersby. Sunny had counted a few complete dousings before calling Spitzer.

"I mean I'll go," she said. "I just don't really even know you, or whose place we're going to, or what to wear."

"The invitation says holiday attire," Sunny said.

"That helps," she said.

Sunny had not considered that he would feel guilty for asking her.

"You don't need to say yes," he told her. "I just assumed it might have something to do with the case, and that you might better recognize any strange behavior, locally speaking. Plus we have things to talk about. Plus I do not want to go alone."

Spitzer sighed.

"No I'll go," she said. "But what is holiday attire, even? Whose holiday? I'm Jewish. Are you picking me up?"

The house was more compound than house, with valets driving guests' cars off to hidden lots so as not to spoil the artifice of polar isolation. The wonderland effect had been embellished by an artillery of Sno-Cannons blasting icy particulate into the clear night sky, which landed on the lawn in unconvincing mounds. An animatronic nativity scene and floodlit sleigh reminded Sunny that he had never been able to reconcile the confluence of wise men and reindeer.

Inside, Sunny and Spitzer strolled through a palatial foyer, grabbing at crab rangoons sailing by on platters. Spitzer pointed out the bar and Sunny scanned the red ribbon and garland-festooned balcony. He was looking for anyone who might have been seeking his attention, but the looks returned to him seemed only to question the whereabouts of attire more festive than the light-up necktie, set to off, that he had bought from a gas station en route. Spitzer wore a black dress with gold accents, which she had claimed to have pulled from the back of her closet despite the tag Sunny had helped her remove in the car, embarrassing them both. Her only holiday tchotchke, a snowflake necklace she had held up to show him, now dangled out of sight.

They cut through the party toward the back, where a crowd of smokers had gathered on the deck. Pinup lights of red and green blinked on and off like warning signals. The long yard sloped down to the lake, where a winterized boathouse sat well above the partially frozen water. A silhouette of mountains stood silent beneath the stars.

"I'm leaving you here," Spitzer announced. "Whoever's looking for you doesn't appear to be looking for me."

She went back inside through a sliding glass door and Sunny took the deck steps down to the lawn. Short grass crunched with frost beneath his shoes and a bonfire burned by the water. Sunny walked down to it and discovered a potbellied man in a Santa hat leaning perilously close to the head-high flames, attempting to light a joint. The white pom-pom of his hat was mere inches from immolation.

"I have matches," Sunny told him.

The man swung his head to face Sunny and adjusted his smoke-afflicted eyes.

"'At's more like it," he said.

Sunny went to his coat pocket for the matches and beside them felt the gift he had brought, a lapel pin of a Modigliani scribble, outlined in gold leaf. Sunny handed the matches to the man.

"I forgot to give my gift," Sunny said. "Do you know if there's a table somewhere?"

"That's later," the man said. "You've never been here."

"I don't even know whose house I'm at," Sunny said.

The man lit the joint and inhaled deeply.

"Funny you're here then," he said, careful to contain the smoke in his lungs, "not knowing where you're at."

"Someone slipped me an invite," Sunny said. "Any chance you might know who?"

The man handed Sunny the burning joint.

"Here," he said. "Take this."

Sunny inhaled and the smoke singed lightly. He pushed it out evenly through his nose.

"Now follow me," the man said.

He marched off toward the boathouse with Sunny in pursuit. A shield of overgrown boxwoods obstructed a side door that Sunny followed the man through. A yacht named *Roxanne* was docked inside on risers.

"Hop on," the man said.

Sunny boarded *Roxanne*. He could hear the light murmur of voices and noticed a faint glow coming from an aft cabin.

"Go in there please," the man said. "And don't worry about it."

"What about you?" Sunny asked.

"I'm coming," the man said. "Just grabbing the bait."

He indicated a refrigerator on the boathouse dock.

"Bait?" Sunny said.

The man turned and debarked the boat. Sunny listened closely for a sense of whom he might encounter. The conversation sounded sparse and easy, and he went down below.

"Here he is," someone said.

Sunny opened the hatch and discovered a well-dressed man and woman seated in the spacious cabin finished with wainscoting and caning, reminiscent to Sunny of an Adirondack fishing lodge, though he had never been in one.

"Hi Sunny," the man said. "Sorry about all the song and dance here. It's just our way. I'm Jim Rolando. Have a drink?"

Sunny gestured his assent.

"Mason, a drink for Detective Shimura, would you?" Jim Rolando called up to the man who had led Sunny there.

"You've already met Mason," Rolando said. "And over there," he said, gesturing, "is my wife, Alva. This is our place you're at. You're very welcome to be here."

Mason came down the steps and attended to a small bar of intricate craftsmanship.

"Tequila okay?" he asked Sunny, though he had already poured it and was now garnishing Sunny's drink with a healthy wedge of lime.

The citrus mixed with the smell of rich mahogany, lacquer, and the appealing imprint of tobacco.

"Have a seat," Rolando said.

Mason handed Sunny his drink.

"I hear that on top of being an art crime investigator, you're also a surf rider," Rolando said. "Tell me, how does one surf in Boston?"

"It's no Bora Bora," Sunny said.

"I'll give you that," Rolando said. "We don't have much surf boarding up here, but we do have other activities on this tremendous lake. It's a wonderful town with wonderful people, Sunny. Respectful people. Smart people. Curious people."

Sunny detected unease in Rolando's voice.

"A nice campus as well," Sunny said.

"We certainly think so," Rolando said. "I'm on the board up there. I chair it, actually. Heard you got over to the Beaumont yesterday, with Eileen."

Sunny was setting some pieces aside and fitting some together to lay out a frame.

"I did," he said. "An impressive collection."

Sunny sipped his drink.

"It's nothing compared with what you're used to down in Boston," Alva said. "We're supporters down there, too. I absolutely love getting lost in those big rooms and hallways. And I always seem to come to the same place, that statue they pulled from the pyramids. The one they used a crane to get into the building."

"*King Nezbura,*" Sunny said.

"Right," Rolando said. "The curators must keep you busy down there. Authenticating and whatnot, making sure you're showing people what they're paying to see."

Mason excused himself and took the steps aboveboard.

"We keep up," Sunny said.

He shook the ice in his drink.

"We're small potatoes comparatively," Rolando said, "but we still care deeply about our integrity."

"I'm sure of it," Sunny said.

"The reason for all of this, Sunny, is that we're interested in keeping this situation you've been briefed on as quiet as we can, understand?"

Sunny said he understood.

"Now I believe we have a mutual friend down at the MFA. He promoted you as an apt detective, Sunny; someone who's particularly sensitive to cases where the appearance of an investigation, or perhaps even the non-appearance, is equally as important as the investigation itself. Does that make sense?"

Sunny told Rolando that it did, though despite their differences, Sunny found it unlikely that Halloway would characterize the detective as a superficial agent.

"Excellent," Rolando said. "Well what's happening here is that a few folks are suddenly convinced that the artwork, this *Humbug*, is no longer the *Humbug* they had before. Now humbug indeed, is what I say. But they seem convinced, and Ms. Spitzer is among them. You already know that though."

Sunny agreed that he did.

"Saint Bartholomew's depends on endowments from donors who recognize its proximity and close ties with the Beaumont's fine reputation as a modest museum with an extraordinary collection. Now I am confident that this talk of forgery and theft is utter horseshit. I really am, Sunny. I know it is. And I know, I really know, Sunny, that any investigation you execute will prove this to be the case. Understand? Because what concerns me most, Sunny, is any word of criminal activity or dishonesty leaking out to our donors. We cannot afford even a shadow of a doubt regarding the authenticity of our collection, detective."

"Have you spoken with Ms. Spitzer directly?" Sunny asked Rolando.

"With Eileen not quite sharing our opinion that everything is as it should be, and with her opinion mattering a great deal on our campus community up here, I'm hoping you might help us convince her that her impression of the situation may be more complicated, or even more simple, than it appears," Rolando said. "She was the one who received the call suggesting the painting was no longer the painting. Frankly I think that call, whomever it came from, just put an idea in her head that she can't shake. Was probably just some student prankster messing around. To some, it looks like trouble, but to others, the painting is just as it should be. Just as it was. What you're doing here, Sunny, I hope, is authenticating that belief."

Sunny heard the vessel's engine sputter on and growl into idle. He looked at Rolando.

"Are we going somewhere?" he asked.

"A little gimmick we do at these things," Rolando explained. "We've got some party favors for everyone stashed in the forecabin. We like to go out, make some noise with a few fireworks, maybe catch a fish or two for the caterers to grill up, and come back bearing presents for all. That reminds me."

Rolando called up to Mason.

"Mason where's that suit?" he said and turned back to Sunny. "Instead of a sleigh we have the *Roxanne*. A little inane, I know, but in the absence of tradition, indignity grows."

He looked at Sunny with the expectation of an enlightened gesture.

"My guest might start to wonder where I'm at," Sunny said. "Perhaps I should stay on shore."

"Nonsense," Rolando said.

Mason came back down with a red, plastic-wrapped Santa Claus suit draped over his arm. Spitzer, looking bewildered, was behind him.

"Hello Eileen," Rolando said. "Welcome to our own sort of North Pole. Care for a drink?"

Spitzer looked at Sunny, who shrugged his surrender to the moment's confusion.

"Whatever that is," she said, pointing at Sunny's glass. "But double."

Soon the boat, isolated completely on the lake in the cold and starlit night, was running at a quick clip to the middle. The cabin undulated in persistent heaves, and Spitzer sat with her arms clasped to the sides of her chair.

"I hate these things," she announced.

"I used to get sick, too," Alva told her, "but now I take something for it."

"That's helpful," Spitzer said, her eyes clenched closed. "Had I known I would be escorted away from the attractive dentist I was getting tennis tips from and led outside onto a fucking boat in December, I might have taken some, too."

"Perhaps some air," Sunny suggested.

A guilty-looking Rolando nodded his support and Sunny led Spitzer to the deck, where Mason, now donned in reefer coat and watchman's cap, stood at the helm, catching the wind. Spitzer leaned against the gunwale facing the black mountains and Sunny watched her, framed against the falling moon. She exhaled deeply and sipped at her drink.

"What was all of that about?" she asked him, her composure returned.

"Feeling better?" Sunny asked.

"I'm completely fine," she said. "I just didn't like being down there. Guy's a worm."

"They just wanted to know how the case was going," Sunny said.

"I bet," she said.

She pulled her jacket tight around her shoulders.

"I may not be seasick," she said. "But I am freezing."

Sunny studied the menu options for his response, but to his great relief, Spitzer chose one for him.

"You can put your arm around me without me hitting you, you know," she said.

Sunny did as instructed.

"Did he tell you that I'm crazy and that the painting's not a fake?" she asked.

"Not entirely," Sunny said. "Though we will have to bring it back to Boston for better analysis."

Mason opened up the *Roxanne* and the wind became so loud that they were yelling, as though calling to each other from distant hills.

"But isn't there more you can do here?" Spitzer asked. "Like detective stuff? Interrogating people and all that?"

"We'll need to get a list together," he said.

"Will I be on it?" she said.

Sunny had to press his hat against his head to secure it in place while holding on to Spitzer. The boat lurched suddenly to a crawl and then a stop, and a blast of sulfurous white light shot from the bow, exploding above them in the sky. Another one followed, sizzling as it climbed and popped. Sparks drifted down to them in a slow, fluttering cadence before fading into the wind. They could hear the party cheering the display from the shore.

"How long will you be gone?" Spitzer asked Sunny.

"Maybe a week," Sunny said. "My boss wants this done quickly."

"Let me know if I can speed things up," she said.

"What do you think happened to the painting?" Sunny asked.

"Is this my interrogation?" she said.

"Reconnaissance," Sunny said.

"Charming," Spitzer said. "What I think is that it's been replaced with a knock-off, obviously. But as far as who painted it, who took it, who replaced it, and who called it in? No idea. But the fact that Rolando's this upset probably means you're striking a nerve. So I guess keep striking."

A soft sequence of Mason's fireworks soared up from the boat and burst above them.

"I prefer them with music," Spitzer said.

Sunny hummed Tchaikovsky, poorly.

The following morning found Sunny and Spitzer standing beside the doors to the Beaumont, watching a team of technicians in white HAZMAT suits and gloves loading a well-wrapped *Humbug* into a windowless panel van. Jim Rolando was indignant at the spectacle.

"This is outrageous," he told Sunny, his finger crooked into Sunny's chest. "I thought I had made myself clear."

"We need to test the pigment, Mr. Rolando," Sunny said. "And layering. You just don't have the equipment here."

"What do you need?" Rolando said. "We'll order it today. It can be here in a week."

"No need," Sunny said. "I should be back by then anyway."

"Tremendous," Rolando said. "Maybe next time you'll bring the armed forces or a military fucking marching band. Fucking Christ."

Rolando turned to address Spitzer.

"I hope you know what a setback you've caused for the college with this, Eileen," Rolando said. "We're really going to have to have some difficult conversations once this blows over."

"Fine by me," Spitzer said. "It all seems to be blowing over quite swimmingly."

She nodded at a police cruiser arriving with its lights on. It pulled in behind the van to escort it back to Boston.

"Fucking Christ," Rolando said again.

TWENTY-EIGHT

Sunny had welcomed the new year alone at a diner, a relic train car overwhelmed by the business district that had sprouted like enormous concrete weeds around it. The houses on Pemigewasset Point were already undecorated and their quiet blandness matched the pallid sea and sky. On this day, an icy broth of kelp and brine inspired no waves. Sunny paddled out regardless, his bare hands and feet conducting the cold. He closed his eyes and listened to the plaintive birdsong of scavenger gulls calling in sequence overhead. When he stopped paddling he hung his arms down, imagining them as bony beacons for any sharks that might have delayed their winter voyage to Florida's continental shelf. He thought of *Humbug*. Though Lang was reputable on the lower tiers of the art world echelon, he was not yet marketable enough to steal. And Sunny did not like the painting.

"Who would want this?" he thought.

A few hours later Sunny was standing in the MFA's research lab with the museum's lead director of provenance, Meg Talbot. The lab had concluded with zero percent uncertainty what Sunny had expected and what Spitzer had told him: that the *Humbug* they had was not Lang's

Humbug. Talbot spoke in a chemist's patois, issuing references regarding dendrochronological investigation, infrared reflectograms, and fluorescent spectroscopy that left even Sunny nonplussed.

"We ran an SEM," Talbot told Sunny, "and detected lead, iron, and cobalt, inconsistent with the artist's other works from that period, as well as with the artist's own description of the paint he used. An optical microscopy confirmed this."

"Ah," Sunny said.

"Also," Talbot said, "chromatography from four different samples all but guarantee that the paint used in the alleged copy is less than a year old."

"Chromatography?" Sunny said.

"Samples from the piece injected into a stream of inert carrier gas and pushed through a heated capillary column so that the molecular components break apart," Talbot explained. "The spectrometer identifies them."

"I see," Sunny said.

"I'm going to theorize a deliberate attempt to deceive here, detective," Talbot said.

"How so?" Sunny asked.

"The ground layers," she said. "The alleged fakist seems to have taken particular steps beyond surface aesthetics to represent the original work."

She walked over to the well-lit table where the *Humbug* lay like a cadaver on a white sheet.

"There's a viridian here that you generally can't buy in the states. It's the same transparent hydrated chromium oxide as any other viridian, so there's no great reason to import this particular brand. It's most likely the brand that the artist used in his original, sold almost exclusively in northern Europe."

"So you're saying it might be the original?" Sunny asked.

"No," Talbot said, "because its timestamp is betrayed"—she extended a collapsible metal pointer and directed it to the northwest corner of the painting—"by this."

She hovered the pointer over a small smear of ultramarine.

"A synthetic was developed in the 1800s, but until then, this particular pigment was extremely expensive to import from the Afghan mines. It comes from the lapis lazuli. Ultramarines swabbed from the artist's other pieces in the series are natural, a general anomaly these days, but an idiosyncrasy that seems consistent across the sample field. This ultramarine is synthetic, a hydrochloric acid test made that immediately clear."

"Couldn't the artist have run out of the real stuff?" Sunny asked.

Talbot savored the question.

"He could have," she said. "But that would mean he finished the painting stateside, and *Humbug* dates back almost ten years. This particular ultramarine is American, distributed exclusively throughout the lower forty-nine. It's common and inexpensive. High school and college art departments often use it. In fact, lab results on this blue match the exact age and chemical structure of an ultramarine tube sampled at the college where the artist was at residence."

Talbot held up the tube in question.

"I'm objectively certain that the paint came from this."

"So you think it was the artist forging his own painting," Sunny said.

"That's beyond my field," Talbot said. "But it's a strong possibility. It's also possible that someone else with access to this paint, I'm thinking students here, would be worth looking into. Though I assume you've already gone through the class list comprehensively."

"I—" Sunny started.

He was relieved to have Halloway walk in and interrupt.

"Hello," Halloway said to Sunny, the latter syllable falling through a tenuous smile. "May I borrow you for a minute?"

Sunny thanked Talbot and followed his boss back through the door. They walked without speaking down the long hallway to Halloway's office.

The office boasted expensively framed prints from exhibition openings, autographed lithographs, and an oversized portrait of the director himself, set in densely applied oils, his face emerging from darkness in a burdened scowl. The real scowl met Sunny in-person a few feet below, though without the portrait's moody context, the grimace looked strained with intent and practiced labor.

"Sunny, I thought you were going to work quickly on this case," Halloway said.

"It's only been a week, sir," Sunny said.

"A week," Halloway repeated. "Exactly. With the report you were just given I would imagine that you have more than enough to wrap this up and move on. The FBI agrees it's going rather slowly."

Sunny did not expect Halloway to be lying outright, but recognized that his superior often misunderstood and thus mischaracterized the inner functions of the bureau, perhaps deliberately.

"They haven't mentioned anything to me," Sunny said.

"Well it seems like we should know something by now," Halloway said. "Jim is very concerned. As well, I need your attention on other things. There's an exhibition opening in June featuring artwork by a motorcycle gang from Malden. They do plein air in the Emerald Necklace and I need a few of them vetted before we can endorse their work."

"There's plenty of time," Sunny said. "Send me their names and I'll get started."

Halloway looked both frustrated and appeased.

"Sunny, I'm going to have to provide you with some help on this," Halloway said.

Sunny despised partners. He stared at Halloway, determining what level of resistance would be appropriate.

"Dr. Gao?" Halloway called to the closed door.

"With all due respect," Sunny started, though Halloway cut him off.

"Dr. Gao is an excellent choice, Sunny," Halloway said. "Where the fuck is he?"

He turned over his shoulder toward the door.

"Gao!" he yelled.

The door opened and a short man with the same long coat that Sunny wore walked through it. Though his eyes were serious, his mouth teetered permanently on the verge of a half-smirk, particularly on the left-hand-side of his face. He presented himself to Sunny with an awkward bow.

Dr. Gary Gao had been sent to the Boston bureau by MIT decades earlier, a mutual benefit to both institutions. The FBI employed Gao while his mind was still in the early years of its long-running brilliance and still susceptible to absorbing and adapting to the bureau's systematic purview. The university, meanwhile, was relieved to offload their experimentally negligent wunderkind before he blew up their labs. He had earned the right not to handle street cases anymore, abetted by his outstanding tenure of failing to interact with society at large without extreme awkwardness and discomfort to himself and his interlocutors. Left to the labs, he buried himself in subatomic research that would require generations of time to prove useful, and even more to render into an invaluable standard of molecular analysis. He took the empty seat beside Sunny.

"You'll travel together this evening," Halloway told them. "Back to New York. I want this closed by the weekend."

He pivoted to address Sunny specifically.

125

"I'm sure you're doing great work on this," he said. "Just speed it up if you can. This all seems a little straightforward for the time that it's taking. And please do remember Jim. This is an extremely fragile matter for him, and Jim is a dear friend."

"We'll have something soon," Sunny said.

"Have everything soon," Halloway said.

It was snowing in Lake Placid and the streets were loud with traffic. The detectives had walked from the motel through the frozen chop and now sat beside each other at a two-tier café. The second floor had been hollowed out and its circular balcony overlooked the coffee bar below. Landsaw sat across from the detectives. He, like Sunny, had ordered a black coffee. Gao was still waiting for a peppermint milkshake. The questioning had begun innocuously: what were Lang's classes like? Was he a fair grader? What interactions did he have with his students?

A group of classmates Landsaw knew came up the stairs with coffees and looked alarmed at Landsaw's obviously police-adjacent guests.

"You guys aren't very good at not looking like detectives, you know," Landsaw told them.

"How we look is irrelevant," Sunny said. "Our intention is simply to find out what your professor was like."

"Not to be rude," Landsaw said, "But if it's irrelevant, why are you both dressed the same?"

"Tom," Sunny said. "What was Professor Lang like?"

"Kind of a prick?" Landsaw said. "He drank a lot and had an ego."

"Did you ever seem him drink?" Sunny asked.

"Sure," Landsaw said. "He had a party one time."

"And who came to this party?" Sunny asked.

"A bunch of us?" Landsaw said. "We got drunk and went swimming. It was fine."

"Did anybody spend the night?" Sunny asked.

"Not that night," Landsaw said. "I mean not that I know of."

A woman and a small dog wearing a flannel jacket that matched its owner's came up the stairs. Gao tapped Sunny's arm and pointed to the dog, smiling at it brightly through his mouthful of gold-capped teeth. While Gao watched the dog, Landsaw watched Gao and Sunny watched Landsaw.

"What do you mean not that night?" Sunny asked.

"I mean I don't know if anybody stayed that night," Landsaw said.

"Were there other times when someone might have spent the night?" Sunny asked.

"I don't know," Landsaw said.

"Tell us what you do for fun," Sunny said.

"Drive around," Landsaw said. "Hang out."

"With whom?" Sunny asked.

"Friends?" Landsaw said. "Should I list them?"

"What did you do before you came here?" Sunny asked. "Why did you go to art school?"

Sunny rested his arms on the table and upset its balance, churning his and Landsaw's drinks out of their mugs. He mopped at the mess with an inadequate wad of small paper napkins.

"I was offered a scholarship," Landsaw said.

"Why?" Sunny asked. "Tell us about Italy."

"That was forever ago," Landsaw said.

"What did you study there?" Sunny asked.

"Painting," Landsaw said.

"What specifically?" Sunny asked.

"Copies," Landsaw said. "Like what we were doing with Lang."

127

A server came up and delivered Gao's milkshake. The detective received the glass and inspected its mint green hue from all angles before discarding the straw and bringing the glass to his lips. He devoured its contents in a single sip while both Sunny and Landsaw watched in mildly disgusted wonder. When he was finished, he wiped his mouth with one of the sodden napkins from Sunny's spill and returned to watching the dog. Sunny returned his attention to Landsaw.

"What do you mean what you were doing with Lang?" he asked.

"The copies," Landsaw said.

Sunny turned to Gao, who tuned back in.

"What copies?" Sunny asked.

"The copies we made of Lang's painting."

"Which painting?"

"*Humbug*?" Landsaw said.

"Are you telling us that you forged Lorcan Lang's *Humbug*?" Sunny asked.

"I am," Landsaw said. "We all did. Me, the kid with crutches who sat behind me, the kid with dandruff who sat next to me, my girlfriend, Julie, and the girl who sat in front of us, whose underwear rode up to like the middle of her back, which we couldn't tell if she was doing on purpose. That was the assignment."

"What assignment?" Sunny asked.

"Am I the first person you've talked to?" Landsaw asked. "Do you really not know about this?"

"Tell us," Sunny said.

"Professor Lang had the whole class copy his trashy painting, or 'picture.' To teach us about authenticity or something."

"This was an assignment?" Sunny asked.

"It was," Landsaw said. "And why are you starting with me? Shouldn't you be going alphabetically or something?"

128

"You mentioned a girlfriend," Sunny said. "Who's that?"

"Julie," Landsaw said.

"Julie White?" Sunny asked. "Where is she?"

"She kind of disappeared," Landsaw said.

Gao looked at Sunny.

"A very suspicious circumstance," Gao half-whispered to his partner.

"Tell us more about that," Sunny said to Landsaw.

"She was here last semester," Landsaw said. "And now she isn't here."

"Do you know where she went?" Sunny asked.

"I wouldn't tell you she disappeared if I knew where she went," Landsaw said.

"And you were dating?" Sunny asked.

"Something along those lines," Landsaw said.

"Tom," Sunny said, "if everyone in the class copied the painting, where are these copies at now?"

"I don't know," Landsaw said. "But Lang kept mine."

"Why yours and no one else's?" Sunny asked.

"Apparently he liked it," Landsaw said.

"Did he like Julie's copy?" Sunny asked.

"I don't know," Landsaw said. "I never saw it."

"Why not?" Sunny asked.

"Because like I said, she disappeared."

TWENTY-NINE

J ulie in the desert."

"Julie somewhere out there."

"The once and future Julie."

The mail went out once weekly and had to be in to Katy Karloff by 10 am. Julie was close to missing the deadline. She settled on a practically scribbled "Julie with a hug" and stuffed her note into the envelope, already addressed to Landsaw, and licked it before she could change her mind. The seal was barely set before she regretted her sign-off. Did it contradict the message? What was the message? She could not remember a line in full. Something about where she was and why she was there. Half-apologies for something. She remembered the futile gesture of her last letter to Landsaw. She walked quickly to the main office and slid the letter through the wooden slot, where it lay irretrievable. *Julie with a hug.* The line burned in her brain for days.

Despite the chill of the morning desert, Julie had adopted the habit of rousing early and setting off to vague destinations. She often selected her route from the farthest point she could see from the office porch, one to which she had not yet hiked. With each long walk her options for endpoints toward which to wander drew increasingly closer, shortening in length and easing in difficulty. Later she would point to show Katy where she had been. A field guide she had bought, semi-studied, and brought with her on these expeditions proved useless. She had no capacity for committing to memory the flora she passed and wished to know by glance. Sage, prickly pear, and chaparral were about all she could identify with any certainty. She was equally inept at birds. She could not remember if a hawk was rare or how to tell one from an eagle. She would stop and watch any large bird that she saw for at least a few moments, so that she would not miss a potentially exquisite encounter, though all birds appeared equally graceful to her, circling the emptiness above her.

The Dead Horn Women's Visual Arts Ranch and Retreat was not exactly what Katy had pitched, though Julie was not yet ready to decide that it was not, either. The verbose name represented Katy's ambition as well as her lack of self-awareness. The only true component of Katy's business title was "ranch." She owned and ran a full stable of horses with which she had used to offer morning and afternoon tours of a nearby canyon, pointing out to tourists indulging their cowboy dreams a scattering of abandoned movie sets and known hideouts of famous gangsters. But as she shifted the focus of her business, she had hired a third-party Dutch franchise to run the tours. Her negotiations had been impetuous, and the contract left her in the care of the horses and stalls, leaving her artists-in-residence to become shit-kickers of no minced words.

The "women" qualifying the title was indeed misleading. While women comprised the majority of artists Katy accepted, as well as the majority of bodies within the boundaries of the sprawling property, the personalities of the male ranchers on the premises compensated for their outnumbering in surfeit. Some of the cowboys were leftovers from another era, while others were just lost. One of them, James, who Julie and the friends she had made theorized was a recently returned and demurely welcomed way-ex-boyfriend of Katy's, seemed to have nothing definitively his own to attend to beyond posing in Katy's office chair with

131

his reading glasses stationed halfway down his nose, flipping through account books that Julie doubted he understood.

James might not have been so bad had he not adopted the habit of asking the artists about their work in ways that debased and enervated their creative inclinations, dumbing down their processes to a digestible mash for his consumption. He would forget anything the artists told him anyway. Julie, sometimes pretending and sometimes sincere, used burying herself in her paintings to avoid any gathering James might attend. And so it was without pleasure that she discovered him one morning outside her cabin door. Her canvas curtain had been rolled up to allow in the morning sun, which she liked to let wake her slowly. James' knock on the frame shook loose the latch.

"Sorry," he said, widening the now open door. "I guess it's broken."

Julie could not remember if James usually wore a bandana around his neck, but if he did, it looked especially foolish on him now. She thought he looked more apt to sell microwaves than swing dick on a dude ranch. And the boots did not help.

"It wasn't before," Julie said, her voice rough from sleep.

She rose from beneath her blankets, taking the top one to cover herself as she met James at the door. She propped a foot to keep him from opening it further.

"Hope I didn't wake you up," he said.

Julie glared at him.

"Someone called and asked that you call him when you can," James said. "Thought you might not want to wait on this one. And I didn't want to tell you in front of everybody. Probably not a big deal, but he said he's some kind of—" James let the word gather in his mouth, "detective or something. None of my business, of course."

He produced a note from his shirt pocket and handed it to Julie. She accepted it and James stepped back and turned to leave, but he stopped in the dirt path leading to her door.

"I don't know what he wants," James said. "But if there's anything we can help with, me and Katy, be sure to ask."

Behind her "Thank you, James," Julie felt ridiculous for hating him, though she did not know if this brief display of consideration would ultimately make her like him any better. The note in her hand distracted her from giving the matter much thought. Its absence of information seemed cruel, and she wondered if James had dropped a page. "Detective Shimura," "questions," and a phone number was all that James had written.

THIRTY

Landsaw snapped the Packard into fourth for the final stretch of frozen washboards the road to Ruth's house had become. The hollow was dark and the hill's sporadic homes were tucked in for the still-early night. He opened the front door to the house and dropped his bag, lapping once around the downstairs before grabbing a beer from the six-pack Ruth had waiting for him in the refrigerator. Soon the bells hanging from the front doorknob clanged with the kick of Ruth's boot, and a rush of cold air preceded his mother calling his name. Her face was flush and she kissed his cheek with the lingering hint of gin.

"I saw your lights," she said. "I can't believe that ridiculous car can make it up here when it's like this."

"Happy birthday," Landsaw said.

"Thank you," Ruth said. "But you know Ron's new boyfriend wrecked his Bentley on the road recently? He says hi by the way."

"I've never met Ron's new boyfriend," Landsaw said. "But tell him hi back."

"Ron says hi, wiseass," Ruth said.

She worked her feet out of her boots and hung her coat on the top corner of the closet door.

"No girl," Ruth said.

"No girl," Landsaw confirmed.

"Invited?" Ruth asked.

"She would have been," Landsaw said. "But she never came back. Sent me a letter from a commune for lady painters or something out west."

"It's a confusing age," Ruth said.

Landsaw was unsure as to whether his mother meant the age Julie was or the still-nascent nineties, which at the time he was unable to characterize with any defining features.

"Scared her off?" Ruth asked.

"Probably," Landsaw said.

"Well if you're going out there you're not taking that goddamned car," she said. "Take mine."

"I hadn't thought of going out there," Landsaw said. "I think the point of her being there is that it's far away from me."

"Let me try that," Ruth said, indicating Landsaw's beer. "I saw them at Gary's and thought they looked interesting."

Landsaw handed Ruth the bottle and she took a reluctant sip.

"Oh, that's good," she said. "Get me one?"

Landsaw turned into the kitchen and Ruth followed him in.

"Ron took me skiing with his new friend last weekend," Ruth said. "Can you imagine? They had this trailside cabin that this guy had rented. Fireplace, Jacuzzi, leather furniture and whatnot. And Ron brings his spinster old neighbor."

"Was he upset?" Landsaw asked. "The new friend I mean?"

Landsaw opened the fridge and retrieved a beer for Ruth.

"We had a wonderful time," Ruth said. "I even tried pot again."

135

"How was that?" Landsaw asked.

He opened the bottle and gave it to his mother.

"Not like they say," she said. "I didn't see any crazy colors or dragon-flies buzzing around or anything like that. It just made me want to dance, and then eat, and then sleep."

"You danced?" Landsaw said.

"Ron has been giving me all of this wonderful music," she said. "Tribal drums and Latin jazz and things like that. Some of it I like a lot but some of it I just have to pretend is good. You wouldn't like any of it."

Landsaw weighed telling Ruth about the investigation, but when he considered the requisite details of the larger context against Ruth's obvious contentment, he decided against it.

"So where are we going for dinner?" he asked Ruth.

"You pick," she said.

"I'm here for your birthday," he said. "I'm not picking."

Ruth chose the restaurant Landsaw knew she was going to choose. They took the Packard, winding down the icy hill and riding alongside an empty streamed that the ebbing winter would soon leave running in a steady churn. They passed the terminals of back roads like their own, roads that ran east and west across the Green Mountain foothills and curved up into dense woodland. The route climbed one final pitch before cresting to reward the aging engine with a slow and modest descent, down into the valley before them, with the lights of the town shining beneath a high-hanging moon.

The restaurant was crowded, but Ruth had known the octogenarian Swiss-transplant owner since waitressing for him after first moving to the then-quiet ski town in the sixties. He cleared them a table near a large window overlooking the lifts. Their server came with menus and introduced herself as Amanda. She was Landsaw's age and wore a large bracelet on her right wrist. The bracelet traveled the length of her bare forearm each time she moved it.

"Well she's something," Ruth told Landsaw after she had gone. "That used to be me, wiggling around in my skinny little jeans like I'd never get old. But here we are."

Landsaw grimaced at the image.

"Your father certainly had my number," Ruth continued. "He could have had any girl in the valley back then."

"I know the story," Landsaw said.

"Well it's my birthday," Ruth said. "I'm allowed a little time traveling. You know that rattletrap you have parked out there is the first car he picked me up in."

"I know," Landsaw said. "I've still never sat in the back seat."

"Might not want to sit in the passenger seat then, either," she said.

"Check please," Landsaw said.

Amanda returned and Ruth ordered an expensive Bordeaux with two glasses. Amanda smiled at Landsaw in lieu of checking his ID and left to get the bottle.

"She likes you," Ruth said.

"I might have liked her back if you hadn't implied that she was you," Landsaw said.

"All the lovesick girls around here are me," Ruth said. "Even before I was. Ask her out?"

"Not there yet," Landsaw said.

"Too bad," Ruth said. "You know you can't just stand against the wall and wait for someone like that to come throw her arms around you. You were lucky with the last one, if you want my opinion."

"Thanks," Landsaw said. "I do not."

The wine came, accompanied by warm bread and softened butter imbued with garlic. Ruth layered a slice and bit in, savoring it.

"Same as always," she told Landsaw.

They ate slowly and paired a supplemental carafe with the remaining bites of their meals. The chef encored with an extravagant slice of *charlotte russe*. In the calm aftermath of their eating, and with the addled buzz of the wine skewing his reasoning, Landsaw was close to telling Ruth about *Humbug*, the fakes, Lang, Julie, and the rest of it, but the diaphanous mirth of the moment diverted him, and the next day, while loading his car quietly, ceremoniously, Ruth dried the dishes and watched her son out the window. His wheels were spinning ceaselessly, desperately as always.

THIRTY-ONE

What kind of a person was he? What did you think of him?" Julie sat across from Sunny and Gao over a plate of rubbery nachos that had been cold upon arrival. They were drinking large fountain root beers from tall plastic cups. The Mexican restaurant was just off the main road, not far from the ranch. After Julie's initial panic from James' note had subsided, reason had returned and she called her parents, who called a lawyer. They had looked one up rather than raising suspicion by asking the few family friends who might have made a recommendation.

"Don't waste money on a good one," Julie had told them. "I haven't done anything. I just don't know what this is yet."

Her parents had hired an attorney from Lone Pine, a groomed and vacant looking man named Cecil Dante. Julie thought of Dante sitting alone in his empty office waiting for the phone to ring, and her dependency on such a person depressed her.

"I didn't think anything of him," Julie told Sunny. "Sort of a jerk I guess?"

Dante whispered something to Julie that Julie could not hear.

"And how was he a jerk?" Sunny asked. "Is there a specific example you can provide?"

A phantom flash of memory brought her back to Lang's room.

"I guess he was selfish," she said. "Maybe not a jerk. But just really confident. I guess I don't know how to answer that. Can we move on?"

"In fact we can," Dante announced with hamfisted assuredness.

Sunny and Gao barely registered the interjection.

"Any details you might provide could help the case significantly," Sunny said.

"I don't even know what the case is," Julie said. "I don't know who I'm helping and who I'm not helping, you know?"

With his plastic straw, Gao stabbed noisily at the ice cubes in his cup. Diners at other tables were turning their heads toward the din.

"It's possible that a piece of art was taken from the gallery associated with your college and replaced with a lesser copy," Sunny said. "A piece by Mr. Lang called *Humbug*. Now we're considering multiple angles, and it's been brought to our attention that Mr. Lang himself had assigned each of his students to copy the painting."

"Picture," Julie muttered.

"Right," Sunny said. "Now I shouldn't be sharing this with you, but it's not impossible that Mr. Lang himself had something to do with it."

Julie, Sunny, and Gao all watched Dante struggle visibly to digest what Sunny had said. After a moment of obvious anguish, the lawyer appeared to short-circuit and abandoned his attempt at comprehension.

"Is that it?" Julie said. "They hire detectives for this? Two of them?"

"Not everywhere," Sunny admitted.

Julie scooped barely unfrozen guacamole onto a limp nacho and pined for whatever anybody else, anywhere else, was eating, or whom they were with. Sunny had given up on his fajitas, which had come from the kitchen not at all "sizzlin'" as promised, but charred to such a degree that each bite offered only a mouthful of soft black slivers. Only Dr. Gao ate with gusto.

"Are you meeting with every student?" Julie asked.

"If we have to," Sunny said. "You were next on the list."

"Who was first?" Julie asked.

"Julie," Sunny said. "Can you tell me about why you chose not to return to St. Bart's?"

"I felt like there was more to learn elsewhere," she said.

"That's fair," Sunny said. "But don't you have friends at school that you miss?"

"Not particularly," she said.

"No boyfriends or anything like that?" Sunny asked.

Julie exhaled her resignation.

"I can't think of anyone," she said.

"How long have you and Tom Landsaw been friends?" Sunny asked.

"You think Landsaw stole the painting?" Julie asked.

"Is that the kind of thing he might do?" Sunny said.

"Not really," Julie said. "I mean no. Didn't you already say you thought Professor Lang had something to do with it?"

"I said that we're working multiple angles," Sunny said. "Did you ever see Tom Landsaw's copy of *Humbug*?"

"No," Julie said.

"Why not?"

"He never showed me. I don't know if he ever finished it."

"When did you see him last?"

"Before winter break," Julie said.

"What did you talk about?" Sunny asked.

"You don't have to answer that," Dante said.

Julie had practically forgotten that he was there.

"Does Mr. Lang have your copy?" Sunny asked.

"No," Julie said.

"Why not?" Sunny asked.

"Because I never made one," Julie said.

"And why not?" Sunny asked again.

"It was a creepy assignment and I didn't feel like it," Julie said. "I think part of me knew I wouldn't go back. But I do need to get back now. To the ranch I mean."

Gao had been studying the laminated dessert menu and looked disappointed when Sunny approved Julie's sudden adjournment.

"Alright," Sunny said. "If that's all that you're willing to share. But if you have anything else, let us know."

Julie tried to exit the booth but Dante sat in her way, unmoving.

"Excuse me?" she said.

The lawyer came-to and stood up. Sunny laid down cash and a sullen Gao returned the plastic prospect of dessert to the table.

THIRTY-TWO

The small breaks broke in chops that cut broadly to the shore, offering Sunny rides long enough for him to forget his exit strategy for a moment and feel the sea surge beneath his board. From his perspective, the shoreline looked the same as it did on any other morning, except for the additional smudge of red on the beach. From a closer vantage the smudge became a heavily blanketed Eileen Spitzer, sitting in a lawn chair and clutching a thermos of hot coffee. Sunny had invited her down under the pretense of observing the museum's technicians working on *Humbug*, disregarding that much of their work had already concluded weeks prior. But Spitzer had accepted the excuse despite its clumsiness, and insisted on rising early with Sunny to watch him surf.

From atop the suggestion of a wave Sunny offered a shaka sign to Spitzer, who returned the gesture with its irony intact. She followed it with her hand circling her stomach. Likewise famished, Sunny paddled in.

Boston held a false sense of early spring, with sunlight reflecting brightly off of street signs and birds diving through the golden lengths of busy blocks. In a torn vinyl booth at Sunny's diner, he and Spitzer faced one another. Spitzer smiled at the specials.

"I'm never leaving," she said.

"They don't have these up north?" Sunny asked.

"They do," Spitzer said. "But they aren't so deliberate, you know? They're just where people get breakfast and read the high school volleyball scores."

Them's "My Lonely Sad Eyes" bounced along in its mid-tempo ballad breeziness from a jukebox at the rear of the diner car.

"Maybe you're not meant for rural isolation," Sunny said. "Delivery at 3 am might be more your speed."

"Either one is isolation," Spitzer said. "I'll take mine with a view."

She ordered two coffees and a short stack of pancakes with strawberry jam. Sunny braved the lobster benedict.

"So let me guess," Spitzer said. "Ireland."

"Ireland?" Sunny said. "What about it?"

"Well aren't you going there?" Spitzer said. "Or do you think you'll extradite him?"

"You mean to talk to Lorcan Lang?" Sunny said. "I'm not sure this case is at the level of extradition. Plus that's the court's decision. But I don't know about going up to Donegal either."

"But the European paint and the blue from the school," Spitzer said. "Who else would have that particular color profile?"

"How valuable is *Humbug*?" Sunny asked.

"It depends," Spitzer said. "The market is basically made up. It's probably tens of thousands? But say he gets a key nod from a certain collector. Something like that could push it up to the low hundreds. And if he dies, probably closer to a million. Contemporary is in, as long as there's bona fide buzz."

Their coffees came and Spitzer unloaded a seconds-long stream of sugar into hers from the dispenser held upturned. Sunny withheld his disapproval.

"And buzz could be anything, right?" he asked. "Including, perhaps especially, theft?"

"Yeah," Spitzer said. "But it would be impossible to sell for a while. Unless," she tapped the table for emphasis, "the painting magically returns to the artist. A trick made far less tricky if the artist already has it. But you're the detective," she said. "That's just what I think. I mean, who else could have done it? And why?"

"Julie White," Sunny said. "Though you didn't hear that from me."

Spitzer choked on her coffee.

"The *girl*?" she said, recovering her composure. "I at least thought you might think it was the *boy*. You know, the one who's famous for copying paintings?"

"You think it might have been him?" Sunny asked.

He regretted the question, embarrassed to reveal that he was grasping at straws to close the case.

"No," she said. "But I think he makes more sense than she does."

Enormous plates of food arrived and Sunny poured syrup onto his.

"Maple syrup on lobster?" Spitzer said. "Very revolting. No offense."

"Halloway won't want me going overseas," Sunny said.

"So maybe we go on our own," Spitzer said. "It's coastal, right? Bring your board."

"We?" Sunny repeated. "If I'm going, you're not. It's too dangerous."

"What's he gonna do?" Spitzer asked. "Whap you with a paintbrush? I bet he'll be relieved. I bet he's in over his head and now he's looking for a way to come clean. Maybe he enters a plea deal or something. Or maybe he writes it off as performance art. I bet he doesn't even see the inside of a jail cell."

145

"You watch too many movies," Sunny said.

"Hardly," Spitzer said. "It's just that I think I know how this one ends."

Sunny mopped at his reservoir of syrup and broken yolk with a forkful of crustacean and impaled English muffin.

"Look," he said. "I would obviously want you to come with me if I went. I think you know that. But bringing you into the case more than you're already involved could derail things when it goes to trial."

Spitzer's feet found Sunny's beneath the booth.

"I hear the Emerald Isle is a cold and lonely place," she said. "Sure you wouldn't want some company?"

"Worry not," Sunny said. "I'd have Gao."

THIRTY-THREE

The case had edged Julie's inability to focus even deeper into self-consciousness, now compounded by angst. Her long walks no longer cooled her feverish worry, and she had begun accepting Katy's neo-Ayurvedic advice to overcome her creative clog, augmenting her diet away from white foods and sitting for frustratingly interminable sessions with singing bowls, crystals, and offerings to planetary deities she did not care much to disturb. But still she sat idle in her cabin studio, her work diminished to an exercise of patience. She watched her blank canvas until the long shadows of the day passed it by. Her general gameness faded to a weary boredom, and she considered going home.

But it was Landsaw's sudden arrival that stopped her. He had driven across the country over a four-day marathon, leaving on the first morning of the spring semester break and camping out along the way. Though far from inspiring the return of Julie's productivity, his presence at least provided someone familiar with which to share her desperate internalizations. To Katy, Julie wrote off Landsaw as an anatomical comfort blanket, helping her conceive the requisite mood for painting. And Katy did not deny the gesture's romantic value, going so far as to consider

Landsaw's arrival the cosmic response to their spiritual summons. Regardless, the full moons that Julie's eyes had become were enough to secure Katy's approval, and with Landsaw's commitment to help shovel shit, she let him stay.

Between the reunited couple there were no questions or a repositioning of the past, there was just what there had been before. They took long drives through open desert and into the valleys of fertile farmland. They explored giant sequoias and the lunar plains of Death Valley. They learned to haul water with them to cool the Packard's radiator and would rest in whatever shade they could find. At an orchard near Twin Oaks they spread a blanket deep in a meadow of Braeburn trees. Julie read and Landsaw watched the sky through the holes in his hat. He lingered into a dream and stayed there until he awoke to Julie's rousing. A black car was coming up the dirt path where they had left the Packard. Assuming they were trespassing, they crouched in the slope of a natural swale and lay hidden, watching the driver as he slowed and then stopped. While they watched, Landsaw's hand traced the curve of Julie's hip to her bare back. The driver got out of his car, leaving his door open as he inspected the Packard. Landsaw feathered the pale suggestion of his fingertips on Julie's skin, daring her to suppress a revealing frisson. She disarmed his challenge with her own, rolling on top of him. While holding him down, she kept watch over the faint rim of their hideout, ducking when she thought they had been discovered. When she checked again, the man had returned to his car and closed the door. He left a long cloud of dust as the car disappeared. Julie watched the dirt lift from the road and catch the last rays of the diminishing sun. She drank in the vast beauty of the empty landscape and sank back down onto Landsaw.

THIRTY-FOUR

Lorcan Lang closed a set of twenty and landed his second dart on a double nineteen. The third one drifted into the board's slice of five, clearing his score. He had yet to make it past fifteen, and barring an intervention from some pub sport deity, his chances of regaining lost ground against his rival's faultless run, presently chipping off his set of twos, were grim. A rainstorm was passing through Donegal and those with money in the game huddled in a corner by a leaky stove to watch. Wind blew the rain in through the street-facing windows. Plywood tables lacquered black sat soaked and chained together outside. Lang's opponent plunged the fatal bull's-eye and turned to the modest bounty they had placed in a hat on a stool. Cigarettes were lit, salutations uttered, and Lang removed himself to smoke beneath the awning of the cobblestone courtyard out back.

As Lang lit up, the door he had come through opened again behind him. The bartender stepped out with another woman he did not recognize, joining him under a small canopy.

"Fuck, I left my bag," said the woman who was not the bartender.

She went back inside and the bartender lit her cigarette and nodded to Lang. She exhaled a lungful of smoke before her deep-set eyes, pale and calm in their resignation of what was all but guaranteed to be an abbreviated life. Her friend returned and Lang watched the rain pour down harder now under the patio lights.

"You hear about Kathy then?" the bartender's friend asked the bartender.

"Kathy which Kathy?" the bartender asked.

"Kathy Norris Kathy."

"Here we go," the bartender said. "What now?"

"Her husband, George? Reads these books. They're in a big series like. Mysteries and murders and whatnot. Well his birthday was coming and she wanted to get him one, but she didn't know which ones he didn't have."

"Okay," the bartender said.

"Well she hoped to have a long look at his shelves without him knowing what she was up to, so she came home on her lunch hour a week or so ago to take a look and write things down, you know?"

"Sure," the bartender said.

"So when she pulls in, she sees the son's girlfriend's car sitting there in the drive. She thinks she'll turn back and let them have their fun, you know, playing hooky and whatnot. But then she hears them. These wild groans coming from an open window. And she's got a nosy neighbor, always airing out everybody's laundry with everybody, so Kathy goes in to break up the business."

"Incredible," the bartender said.

"Just wait," her friend said. "So she goes to her son's bedroom, but she doesn't find them in there, so she follows the panting to her and George's room, and when she opens the door, who's in there but George and the girlfriend, writhing around on the bed. And they've got this birthday cake smeared all over themselves."

"That's not real," the bartender said.

"Is so," the friend said. "The cake was sitting out on a side table with a knife in it. So everyone's looking at one another, not knowing what to do. George tries to mutter some kind of excuse to Kathy and Kathy's thinking she'll go for the knife, but what she does instead is she goes for his books. They're hard backed and all, these things, like bricks. And so she gathers a few and starts tossing them. Not even tossing, but like hurling, you know? Throwing really hard, right at them. Accuracy she didn't know she had. George is covering his head, Kathy's going for his ribs. He covers his chest, so she gets him in the head. On this one throw she drills him square in the teeth and blood flies out everywhere. By now, the girl is up and off over in the corner trying to get back into her clothes, but Kathy wings one at her, too, not just for getting dirty with George but for messing around behind her kid, you know? And the girl goes down, stone still and blank on the carpet. Kathy wonders if she isn't dead, but empties the entire bookshelf at the both of them regardless. When she runs out of books she sees her room there, all awash with cake and blood and those pages, with George screaming through a mouthful of smashed teeth and the young plaything just lying there lights out with her pants half-on."

"Jesus," the bartender said. "Bloody awful."

"Isn't it?" the friend said. "Anyway, George and Kathy are splitting up."

"And the girlfriend?"

"What of her?"

"Well, is she dead?"

"You know, I never asked," the friend said. "But Kathy didn't mention it, so I wouldn't think so."

Lang had had to light another cigarette to hear the full denouement.

"Tremendous," he said.

"Tremendous?" the bartender said. "Kathy's a friend of ours. And anyway she wasn't telling it to you."

"It's still a bloody riot," Lang said.

"It's devastating for everyone is what it is," the friend said. "Who is this then?" she asked the bartender.

"A fucking artist," the bartender said. "Ignore him."

The women snubbed out their cigarettes and turned back inside.

"Devastating for everybody," Lang repeated to himself. "Mercy me."

He threw his cigarette onto the stones and walked back through the door before going out the front. He pulled his hood up against the rain.

Back inside the pub, Dr. Gao sat alone at a corner table, considering the horses, birds, and harps embossed on his Irish pounds. He returned all but a coin to his coat pocket and walked to a payphone in the breezeway.

The room that Sunny and Gao had rented offered a view of Lang's flat. After Gao's call came through, Sunny waited and then watched the lights in Lang's rooms switch on. He met Gao across the street and gained access to the lobby of Lang's building by the luck of a stubborn latch snagged open. They were halfway up the narrow stairs when Lang appeared at the top, tipped off by their clatter.

"Fuck's sake," he said.

He let in the detectives, eyeing them angrily as he held the door.

Lang's apartment was large and soft green drapes were drawn against the night beyond the windows.

"Just a moment then," he told the detectives.

He disappeared down a hallway and Sunny turned to consult Gao, but a Felix the Cat clock on the kitchen wall consumed his partner's attention, its tail swinging out the seconds. Lang emerged moments later with Landsaw's trash bag-covered canvas in his arms.

"Supposedly this is what you came for," he told them.

Lang removed the bag from the *Humbug*.

Sunny registered the painting's vibrancy, contrasting remarkably from the fake left at the museum.

"I hope this helps you find my picture," Lang said, though he was improvising. "Do detectives drink?"

He walked to a kitchen counter and held up a bottle for their approval.

"This isn't your painting?" Sunny asked.

Lang filled a single glass with a substantial pour and took it for himself.

"I'll pretend I'm not offended by that supposition," he said. "This picture was made by an adolescent nitwit, and your folks in white coats will tell you the same. Inconsistencies everywhere."

"Which student painted this?' Sunny asked.

"That Landsaw," Lang said.

"And did he give this to you?"

"He did," Lang said.

"Professor Lang," Sunny said. "I'm going to ask if we might borrow this artwork from you."

"And I'm going to tell you to piss off," Lang said. "An important work of mine has been taken, and you have nothing better to do than to fly across the ocean to harass me and take my things?"

"We were hoping that your cooperation at this point in the case might assist you later on," Sunny said. "If necessary."

"And what precisely are you threatening me with?" Lang asked. "I told you where this copy came from."

"We'd just like to take it with us for verification," Sunny said.

"Balls to your verification," Lang said. "It's mine."

His heart jumped at the careless declaration.

"Strictly in the sense of ownership, mind you," he added. "And I don't readily surrender what's mine. Show me the proper papers if you're so set on taking it. Not that I understand at all how it might help you find my picture. You know bloody well what it looks like."

Sunny signaled to Gao.

"We'll do just that," Sunny said to Lang.

Lang looked relieved.

"But don't come back tonight," he said. "I'm turning in after this."

He held up his glass and drained it, and Sunny nodded his agreement to return in the morning. Lang led the detectives back to the entrance and held the door for them.

Once they were gone, Lang waited an hour before fleeing with the painting, out through a service door at the rear of his building. He had wrapped the canvas in brown paper and handled it like the masterwork of his that he mistook it to be. He boarded a train to Dublin where he found a red-eye to New York, leaving within the hour. The flight was a stroke of serendipity Lang felt he deserved.

He arrived at dawn and took a room in midtown, where he slept poorly with the light leaking through the blinds. He left the *Humbug* in the hotel and went out to purchase his disguise: dark sunglasses; white sneakers; a Yankee's cap; and a knee-length trench coat like Sunny and Gao's. He would stop shaving. He toured Central Park and sat at the water's edge in the Ramble to watch black locusts maneuvering in the wind. After he caught a cab back to his room to retrieve the *Humbug*, he walked with it to Grand Central, where the sounds of the station played off the marble arches leading to the platforms. Lang looked up to find Aquarius inverted in marine, suspended in sidereal splendor.

From his train car window Lang watched a reluctant spring blossoming in the dusk. He read *Henry IV* beneath an overhead lamp, the betrayed Falstaff claiming the utmost of his sympathies. Lang was among the few riders remaining when the train pulled into Lake Placid. A taxi

154

took him to the motel near the campus, where he slept deeply. He awoke the following morning to find the small town draped in heavy fog.

"Wolf Man weather outside," the motel clerk told him.

"I'm in 121," Lang said. "Don't turn the room."

"Hell," the clerk said. "Don't need to tell me twice to not do something I don't even wanna do once!"

Lang smiled at her voluminous laughter and left on foot toward the house where he had previously confronted Landsaw. The new students living there told Lang that Landsaw had moved. Lang hoped the students, sitting in a collective hypnosis around a square of sectional couches, would not recognize him, but the stale stench of pot smoke reassured Lang that if they had known him, they were not apt to recall.

"Might I ask where he moved to?" Lang asked.

"No idea, man," one of them said.

"Try the school office or whatever," another said.

"Very well," Lang said. "As you were."

Lang had never visited the administrative offices of St. Bart's, so he felt there should be no reason for anybody there to know him or his tell-tale brogue. He trusted his unlikely clothes to cover him from former colleagues, all of whom, excepting the Ponds, had kept their distance. Lang had not expected to see the campus in its green and dew-strewn abundance ever again. The early fog was lifting to reveal the mountains beyond the red brick boundaries. There were no students about, and Lang assumed they were still sleeping or tumbling over one another in their darkened dorms.

In the office he discovered a man with a shaved head who Lang thought looked like a sidelined marine. He was standing behind a tall wooden counter.

"Morning," the man said, his stentorian bellow too loud for the time of day.

"Yes," Lang said, suddenly unnerved and speaking softly. "I'm a professor here and—"

"I can't hear you," the man said.

"What?" Lang said.

"I said I can't hear what you're saying to me," the man said. "Speak louder, please."

The man trained a direct stare on Lang.

"Yes," Lang said. "Excuse me."

He cleared his throat and tried again.

"I'm a professor here and I have work from a student that I need to return to him."

The man behind the desk nodded his comprehension, apparently satisfied with Lang's renewed tone.

"I was wondering if you might be able to provide me with his address," Lang said. "Locally, that is."

"What's your name?" the bald man asked.

Lang inhaled.

"John Berger?" he said.

"And the student?" he asked.

"Landsaw," Lang said. "Thomas."

"Just a moment," the man said.

He turned to browse through a drawer of files and picked one from the middle before reaching for a form on a shelf. He placed the form down in front of Lang.

"Fill this out," he said.

While Lang scribbled uncomfortably, he felt the militant man's eyes on him. He signed the adopted name and laid the form on the counter.

The man took it and disappeared into another room. Lang watched the clock above a window. After a moment, the man returned.

"Look these over," he said, passing Lang a sheet with Landsaw's information.

Lang smiled and established eye contact with the clerk for as long as he could bear.

THIRTY-FIVE

The lashing from Halloway was more humane than Sunny had anticipated. While he transferred the assignment of unearthing Lang and *Humbug* to the bureau's missing persons unit, he directed Sunny to consider the case as good as closed: Lang was their man, and the painting would likely be recovered.

Sunny and Gao were meanwhile reassigned to their less-engulfing beats. While Gao began a series of critical treatises that would become a foundational tenet of the forthcoming century's revolutionized lab theory, Sunny returned to the street, particularly the red brick conjunction of Battenkill and Mt. Auburn, in Cambridge, where a line was forming outside of the Battenkill Theatre. Glenn Boone's *Man of Mangani* was advertised in large letters on the small marquee. Inside, Sunny found C. Blake Seward behind the counter with his staff, filling sodas and buttering bags of popcorn. He was working quickly with his head down, securing lids on paper cups, dispensing candy boxes from the glass counter case, and accepting cash from the moviegoers anxious to claim their preferred seats. Between customers Seward glanced up and saw Sunny in the lobby, unmistakable in his coat far too heavy for the warm spring day. He transferred his line to an employee and motioned for Sunny to meet him beside the counter.

"I thought you weren't a movie person," Seward told Sunny.

"Did I tell you that?" Sunny said.

"No," Seward said. "It's just what I had been told."

"I forgot how anticipatory this all is," Sunny said, indicating the busyness of the lobby.

Seward smiled at the orchestrated excitement.

"Come with me," he told Sunny.

Sunny followed him around a corner and Seward unclasped a red velvet stanchion rope cordoning off a winding flight of stairs. Seward sent Sunny up first and refastened the rope behind them. At the top was a projection booth, where a film student had already laced the film through the mass of complex machinery, which took up most of the room.

"I've got it from here, Bill," Seward told the projectionist. "Thank you."

Seward unfolded a metal seat for Sunny and a quiet bell chimed when a big clock above them struck two. Seward pressed a green button and the theater lights dimmed. A lamp on the projector lit and scratches scrolled to life on the screen. Seward focused the projector on the studio logo and took a seat beside Sunny.

"I never show previews," Seward told Sunny. "Bad for business indubitably, but I find them inadequate for whetting the appropriate appetite for a film."

"Must audiences' moods be so primed for Tarzan?"

Seward laughed.

"This is beyond Tarzan," he said. "It's Tarzan as archetype, confined within the shackles of the present-day everyman after fleeing the chaos of the jungle."

"I should be taking notes," Sunny said.

"This is a complicated picture," Seward insisted.

"And I hear Glenn Boone is a complicated actor," Sunny said.

"I should lend you my researchers," Seward said. "Complicated doesn't begin to scratch the surface."

They sat quietly while Seward savored the opening titles announcing his lost lover's presence.

"It was all so ludicrous," Seward said evenly after a while. "Wasn't it?"

"Misguided perhaps," Sunny admitted. "You knew I couldn't have helped."

"Even so," Seward said. "I was deranged into thinking you might."

On screen, Boone swung down into view from a vine in ten-foot Technicolor.

"Of course it wasn't until the thing was actually sitting in my apartment that I thought, what the hell have I done? So I gave up what I was trying to do and just let it be what it was."

"You almost tried to frame him when I met you," Sunny reminded Seward.

Boone was giving chase to a cheetah, smashing through jungle fronds while anacondas slithered in the foreground, raising their diamond heads to the calamity.

"Almost," Seward said. "But I couldn't. I'm a lousy thief, and Glenn never made sense to pin something like this on. He could barely make a dinner reservation without fouling it up. And plus he didn't have any money back then. You know moving a statue like that is expensive, but manageable if you've got the resources."

"Again, Mr. Seward," Sunny said. "I believe it's incumbent upon me to inform you of your rights."

"Don't bother," Seward said. "I know what they are. And they're useless. Can we just watch until the middle? I'll have Bill take over at intermission."

Sunny acquiesced and soon the reel's first cue flashed on the screen. Seward stood and readied his hands to switch the projectors. He executed the changeover at the mark and unspooled the first reel from the machine to cue up the third.

Before them, the thoroughly modern and sophisticated urbanite ad executive Jane, played by Geena Davis, was teaching Tarzan to drive, scuttling along the Pacific Coast Highway in her yellow Stingray. The blue Malibu waves crashed on the empty beach beneath them, where the lovers would inevitably find themselves at the end, rolling in the tide in amorous embrace. The strings would play them out, but Seward would not be watching.

En route to the station, Sunny detoured past Seward's apartment, where a crane was coned off, blocking a lane of traffic. The press had gathered and flashed their cameras high above their heads, where Housemann's *Bottom* hung suspended, bound in ropes and ratchet straps. A flatbed idled nearby. Seward's eyes traced the contours of the hovering statue one last time as it traveled the early evening air, fluttering weightlessly down to earth.

THIRTY-SIX

Two broken bicycles and an overturned plastic bin littered the porch of Landsaw's apartment. An old carpet lay rolled up and rotting in the corner, and cigarette butts spilled from an ashtray flooded with rainwater onto the seat of a wooden lecture hall chair. The metal screen door had no screen, so Lang knocked through it. It occurred to him that Julie might be in there with Landsaw. He tightened at the prospect of facing her again, but the arrival of a figure that was neither Julie nor Landsaw calmed him. A freshly awoken student opened the door and stood utterly naked before Lang, unabashed against the day. He offered no greeting beyond rubbing his eyes.

"Right," Lang said. "Good morning."

"Morning," the student said.

His breath in Lang's face smelled like a toxic spill.

"Is Thomas here?" Lang asked.

"Landsaw?" the student said. "No I don't think so."

"Whom might you be?" Lang said.

"Are you selling something?" the student asked.

"On the contrary," Lang said. "Returning something. To Thomas."

"I'm Jeremy," Jeremy said.

"Okay, Jeremy," Lang said. "Might you know where Thomas is?"

"With his girlfriend, I think," Jeremy said. "Out west."

Lang considered a more frustrated response to this news, but withheld his temper and asked Jeremy if Landsaw's girlfriend's name was Julie.

"Yeah," Jeremy said. "Are you his dad?"

"Sure," Lang said. "I mean yes. I mean I'm his stepdad. I have something I need to give him."

"Well I think they're in Arizona or New Mexico or something like that," Jeremy said.

"Do you know which?" Lang asked.

"Ashley!" Jeremy yelled suddenly.

Lang waited.

"Ashley!" Jeremy yelled again, his eyes turned toward the staircase behind him. "Where did Landsaw say his girlfriend's thing was?"

"What thing?" said a groggy voice wafting down the steps.

"That art thing."

"California," Ashley said sleepily.

"They're in California," Jeremy told Lang.

"Might she know where in California?" Lang asked. "I gather the state is rather expansive."

"Where in California?" Jeremy yelled. "He gathers the state is expensive!"

Lang stifled his correction.

"In the desert," Ashley yelled, now mildly more alert. "A thing for painters. But it's girls only, Landsaw said I think. Who's here?"

"Landsaw's dad!" Jeremy yelled.

"Stepdad," Lang mouthed.

"Stepdad!" Jeremy yelled.

"Oh hi, Mr. Landsaw!" Ashley called down.

"Hello up there," Lang said.

He settled with what he had gleaned and turned back to Jeremy. "You've been helpful," he said. "Please go enjoy your morning."

He winked at Jeremy, who did not register the insinuation.

"Okay you too, Mr. Landsaw," Jeremy said and closed the door.

Within an hour, Lang was checked out from the motel and at the helm of a rented Oldsmobile Cutlass, driving the New York State Thruway with the *Humbug* buckled into the shotgun seat beside him. He sipped intermittently from a Bushmills in his breast pocket and absorbed the greening scenery speeding past him out the windows. An informational booth at a rest stop in Ohio showed images of the once-burning Cuyahoga. On the Mississippi, tankers moved coal beneath the bridges built for oil trains. Lang crossed the Missouri into Nebraska just after midnight and stopped in North Platte, where he encountered a two-story Buffalo Bill fashioned out of plywood, towering over a parking lot. In cartoon lettering the installation told of the famous cowboy showman's murderous tendencies toward his namesake prairie beast, enumerating his kills in the tens of thousands. Lang pissed behind the rigging and slept uneasily in the reclined front seat of the rental. In the rising sun, the wooden cowboy icon's shadow stretched out over him.

Lang breakfasted at the Hi-De-Ho on a downtown stretch of storefront. A photo plaque in the vestibule honored the recently crowned Miss Nebraska, a smiling North Plattian teenager with elaborately manipulated hair crowned with sparkling tiara. The severity in her eyes sent out their own sort of Buffalo Bill agenda. He ate quickly as Hank Williams walked the floor on the radio behind the griddle.

Continuing on, he crossed into Wyoming in a five-hour blur, missing the steep cut south through Fort Collins and defaulting to Salt Lake

City, with a slash down central Utah's mountainous towns—Filmore, Sulphurdale, Pintura—until finally into Nevada and Las Vegas, its desert-jewel radiance the antithesis of the engulfing dark that defined its blaring brilliance. Lang detected the sharp char of spent transmission as he handed the keys to a valet at the Desert Inn.

He hid the *Humbug* in the closet of his room on the sixth floor, overlooking the strip, before ravaging the minibar. He turned the TV on loud and listened to the history of the Hoover Dam from beneath a hot shower. Later, in the hotel's lounge, he soaked steak in eggs and ketchup and drank scotch neat. Monitors encircling the bar above him flashed out basketball games and horse races that had aired hours earlier.

Out in the hot and windless night, the sound of traffic was a jarring contrast to the hotel's illusory circus noise of gambling, which had proved useful in distracting him from what it was that he was up to, though he remained hard-pressed to know exactly what that was. He walked quickly to a neighboring casino. Slot machines were lined up in tidy, ringing rows on the gambling floor, their wheels and tables spinning blurs with high hopes that they would stop on slim chances. Lang tried a dollar he had neglected to forfeit as a tip at breakfast and lost it immediately. A woman in a bedazzled bowtie and little else came around with drinks.

"Excuse me," Lang said, helping himself to a pre-mixed gin ricky.

"Yes?" the woman in the bowtie asked.

Her eyes were painted in an elaborate diorama, smudged slightly from perspiring.

"What can one do here?" Lang asked her. "I mean besides this."

He gestured at the machine before him, displaying a single cherry and two stars, misaligned behind the bulletproof glass. The woman maintained the trained charm of dumb resplendence, pivoting her weight and balancing the almost full tray of warming cocktails against her sequined side.

"Well, what do you mean?" she asked. "Do where?"

Lang looked around the room.

"Here," he said. "Right here. All of this."

He waved vaguely at the ringing machines and blaring neon, muted by a stale fog of cigarette smoke.

"Oh you don't gamble," she said. "I see. Well there's shows. David Copperfield, Siegfried and Roy, Penn and Teller? Maybe magic suits you more than luck does."

The leftover twang of someplace skewing southeast from there punctured the measured mirage of her costume.

"And there's dancers, singers, shopping…is this your first time here?"

"It is," Lang said.

The server looked thrilled.

"Well what do you like?" she asked.

"Beauty," Lang said.

"Oh," the server said, the syllable morphing her practiced smile into an honest smirk. "I get it."

Her voice dropped the remaining residue of artifice.

"Listen," she said. "We don't do what you're lookin' to have done. Try the bar."

She nodded at a woman sitting alone by the server station. She was probably Lang's age but presented herself as younger, wearing a red dress a size-and-a-half too small and nursing water in a rocks glass, embellished with a lime to look like booze. Lang turned back to explain that sex had not been what he meant, but she was gone, and Lang was alone on the floor. For a moment he considered joining the woman at the bar under the pretense of conversation, but when he imagined the acidic flavor of borrowed skin, he went back outside into the night instead.

He walked without direction, passing the twinkling monoliths named for the natural landscapes they had displaced: The Sands, The Dunes, the Oasis and Mirage, each an homage to the vacancies lying dormant beneath their facades. Lang walked to the strip's southern terminal, where a new resort with poolside villas flanked with palms and an ornate fountain of dancing jet streams coordinated to Vivaldi signaled vague roots of European grandeur. It was approaching midnight when Lang walked in. This lobby boasted a sinuous moat with gondolas sailing past cafés and boutique stores, set along the perimeter. Only the customers wandering agog in their sneakers and polos betrayed the otherwise detailed illusion of exclusivity.

Lang looked around for this hotel's iteration of the cocktail server and found her punching in numbers at a register by the foreground of a fake Rialto. But an entranceway he saw through a glass balustrade of the balcony above him diverted his attention. Letters embossed in false marble above the set of double doors boasted Great Art by European Masters. Lang rode the escalator to the balcony and entered the exhibition.

A wall of introductory copy provided a cursory overview of the Renaissance, its creative supernovas, and the impressionist on-ramp to modernity. The gallery was empty but for the paintings and some glassed-off sculptures, stationed in the centers of two long chambers, adjoined in an evenly limbed L. In lieu of classic white, the walls were a deep chartreuse. Newly laid imitation spruce flooring clenched into its epoxy beneath Lang's feet.

Lang approached a Matisse he knew. From a golden frame a woman stared out at him; his gaze was not invited. She wore anatomically impossible folds of red pants and sat on the floor beside an open box and a vase of flowers. Crude green stripes dominated the vertical field in broad bars. The floor repeated the gesture more delicately in the southeast corner. Lang corrected the accompanying placard.

"*Post*-impressionist," he told the wall.

Farther down was a Holbein, similar to his *Ambassadors* with the figure's ostentation and the presence of a skull, though the skull here lacked the right anamorphic skew. A distinguished man in a leopard print scarf held a carafe in one hand and rested the other on the skull's crown as he stared out evenly with admonishing eyes. The slight suggestion of a grin energized his lips. A coat of arms adorned the top-left corner.

"I know you," Lang said. "You're not supposed to be here."

He moved down a pace to a Modigliani featuring a woman with vacant eyes, cocking her head. The painting had no life beyond its crudeness.

Lang turned to address a Vermeer and then a Picasso. He studied a Rembrandt and then a Degas, a Turner and then Manet, the café piece with the artist interrupted.

"Unbelievable," Lang said.

"They are, aren't they?" said a docent whom Lang had not previously noticed.

The impatience in his inflection suggested that he was used to managing drunks from the strip.

"Are you an art lover?" the docent asked him, disguising his antipathy not at all.

"What's going on here?" Lang asked.

"You're in an art exhibition, sir," the docent said. "These are paintings."

"Bullocks," Lang said. "These are fakes. Or else they're stolen."

The docent's demeanor changed abruptly, though he maintained a strained smile to front the heavy discomfort suddenly amassed behind it.

"Excuse me?" the docent asked.

Lang walked up to him and stood close to the young man's face.

"Whose are these?" Lang asked.

"The hotel's?" the docent said.

"Who's your boss?" Lang asked. "I need to speak with someone better than you."

The docent seemed to consider a rote retort, but Lang's glare left him reaching for his radio.

"This is Conway," the docent said into the Walkie-Talkie that had been clipped to his belt.

"Go ahead," someone's voice buzzed through.

"There's a gentleman here asking about the paintings," Conway said.

There was a pause before the radio buzzed back.

"So tell him about them," the voice said finally.

"It's just that he has questions," Conway said.

"What questions?"

"Like about where they came from?" Conway said.

After a moment a hidden door opened and a large man in a dark suit and loud shoes stepped into the gallery. Conway put away his radio as the man approached them.

"What is it?" he asked Conway.

"Who are you?" Lang asked him.

"Cole Michaels," the man said. "The floor manager. And who are you?"

"Lorcan Lang," Lang said. "The artist."

"And what can we help you with?" Michaels asked.

"None of the artworks you're displaying here are real," Lang said. "Or else they're stolen."

Michaels considered Lang evenly.

"Before we continue this conversation," he said. "I need to know whether or not you're hallucinating or if you've taken anything that our medical staff should be prepared to address."

Michaels' tone indicated that the question was sincere.

"Your collection here is all loot and bullshit fakery," Lang said again.

"Alright," Michaels said. "In here, please."

He ushered Lang back through the hidden door and nodded the approval of his summons at Conway. Behind the door was a small room with a desk and two folding chairs on either side. Michaels invited Lang to sit down, though Michaels continued standing.

"Remind me what your name is," Michaels said.

"Lorcan Lang," Lang said.

"And who are you, generally speaking?"

"I told you," Lang said. "An artist. An educator. If you knew anything about art you might know who I am."

Michaels absorbed the antagonizing.

"And remind me what your concern is," he said.

"I know these pieces," Lang said. "The real ones. And these aren't them. Whether it's intentional or not, what you have here is amoral."

"Your dignity is inspiring," Michaels said. "But Mr. Lang, Las Vegas draws millions of visitors each year with an incredible assortment of attractions. Morality is not famous for being among them."

"But the law still applies," Lang said. "And these paintings are illegal."

"Let me ask you something," Michaels said. "How did you get in here?"

"Get in where?" Lang said. "This room? You swept me in like some thug ripped from the funnies. What's the matter with you?"

"I mean this exhibition," Michaels said. "The casino. How did you get here? At any point between wherever the fuck you're from and here, did we, the owners of this collection, ask anything of you? Have you exchanged any money or signed any contract in order to wander up here?"

Lang let his silence respond.

"So what are we selling?" Michaels continued. "Who are we cheating? You doubt the authenticity of these works, that's fine. Personally, I don't. But say a few of them aren't completely original. Say some Latvian fakist mocked them up and sent them over. What is it that you think we owe you or the other people who come in here? Tell me again about illegal."

"You're wiping your ass with integrity," Lang said. "Whoring out authenticity."

"Do you know where you are?" Michaels said. "Do you understand what any of this is? Do you really think the gondoliers downstairs are Venetians who don't go home to drug habits and smashed-up double-wides? Do you think the strippers in the moat are really mermaids?"

"I didn't see those," Lang admitted.

"Well they're there," Michaels said. "And they're fake, too. They're here for Dick and Mary Johnson from Fuckstown, Ohio to look at, not for Mr. Artist with whatever fucking accent that is to whine about and make dangerous accusations that he doesn't seem to understand. Got me?"

Lang sat quietly.

"What are you doing in Las Vegas, Mr. Lang?" Michaels asked.

"I'm looking for my son," Lang said.

"And where is he in Vegas?"

"He's in California," Lang said. "Where I'm headed. An artists' retreat, out in the desert."

"Dead Horn?" Michaels said.

"Perhaps," Lang said. "He's visiting his girlfriend."

"Dead Horn then," Michaels said. "It's the only one I know of. Women artists only."

Lang brightened.

"Yes," he said. "That sounds right then."

"It's a few hours' drive," Michaels said. "Why don't you go back to your hotel, get some sleep, and leave Las Vegas first thing in the morning? There's a lot of desert out there, and I would hate for you to go missing."

Michaels reopened the door and held it for Lang, who stared down Conway once more before exiting the gallery and riding the escalator back down, his eyes scanning the moat for the supposed mermaids.

Back at the Desert Inn, Lang retrieved the Dead Horn address from a concierge and left immediately to drive through the burgeoning dawn. The day's new sun blinded him in the review as he drove past alien rock formations, navigating the remnant roads of abandoned pioneer towns pocked among Death Valley. He shuffled a map against the steering wheel as he drove, tracing the arid hills through Swansea. He checked into a room at a motel in Lone Pine and slept through the morning. He awoke in the late afternoon to find a café, where he ate a burger called the Jackalope. He drank three cold bottles of Mexican beer. The air conditioner was set to high and the staff wore matching Stetsons. On a paper placemat, Lang drew abstractions with a peeling crayon. A dog was barking outside beyond the steel-barred windows, and Lang could see that it was beginning to rain.

THIRTY-SEVEN

J ulie had drunk some but Landsaw had drunk more, so Julie was
driving. As the rain fell hard and pooled on the dirt roads, Julie
gripped the Packard's wheel tightly, crooking out her elbows
with her head craned toward the windshield. Landsaw lit a spliff he had
rolled in the bathroom of the bar using a borrowed pouch of Bugler and
the last few pinches of some crumbly weed Julie's friend at Katy's ranch
had sold him. He switched on the radio but Julie said to turn it off.

"Just softly," he said and turned the dial down.

"You can't even hear it over the rain," Julie said.

"I can a little," he said.

Landsaw scanned the channels and found a station playing bebop.

"Perfect," he said and handed the spliff to Julie, who shook her head
no and steadied the wheel.

The day that had been golden red was now steady gray, the storm
having extinguished the desert rocks glowing in their unearthly ember,
which Landsaw and Julie had been mixing paints to match. The heavy
rain's arrival had sent them to the bar.

"Doing swell, Drool," Landsaw said.

"I can't see shit," she said.

"Want me to try?"

"You can't see shit either," she said.

Landsaw dragged on the spliff and nodded in quiet agreement. He curled the smoke out from his mouth and into his nose, exaggerating his expression and holding it for Julie to see.

"Do I look weird?" he asked.

"I'm not looking," she said.

"I'm doing the French inhaler thing," he said.

"Then yes," she said.

They approached the road to Dead Horn as lighting struck the darkening landscape. The rain beat harder on the windows and appeared to fall sideways.

"Almost there," Landsaw said.

Julie turned onto the road, downshifting for the narrower, more undulating grade. Rainwater filled the packed dirt's pockmarked divots that had washed out to the size of small craters.

"Take them slowly," Landsaw instructed.

The sand held firmly beneath the tires until Julie and Landsaw came to a stream of runoff that had jumped its track and now drained out across the road. The surge gushed over their path with a muddy and expanding pool of indecipherable depth.

"Jesus," Landsaw said.

Another car was pulled to the side of the road before it.

"Who's that?" Landsaw asked.

"I don't know," Julie said. "But we should do the same. There's enough room to pull up behind it."

"No way," Landsaw said. "We can get through."

"Landsaw," Julie said. "No."

"She'll drown out here," Landsaw said. "Or else get washed away. We don't know how long this will last."

"I'm not driving through that," Julie said.

"Then I will," Landsaw said.

"If we get stuck and *she* dies or something that's not on me, okay?"

"Of course," Landsaw said.

Julie lifted herself up over Landsaw as he slid beneath her into the driver's seat. He clasped his seatbelt and shifted back into first, depressing the clutch hard against the floor.

"Put yours on, too," he told Julie.

She did, and Landsaw punched the gas while relieving the clutch. He stomped it back down to hit second and they shot past the parked car and into the rushing runoff. The engine sang and they entered the pool with the wheels slowing to an uneasy crawl. Landsaw corrected his shifting toward the center and they regained momentum, with the Packard lurching forward in jolts. Julie sat straight and unblinking, her fingers pressed hard into her thighs.

"Got it, got it, got it," Landsaw said, the now extinguished spliff bouncing with his bottom lip.

The Packard's front tires caught on the pool's far edge and the sudden traction launched them forward. In the manic release of speed, Landsaw lost control of the wheel and the car sped toward a bank of sand flanking the right side of the road.

"Shit shit shit," Landsaw said, regaining the wheel.

He overcorrected and they bounded now toward the opposite bank. A figure dove to escape the Packard's path and Julie screamed. Landsaw kicked at the brakes, but the body passed beneath them with thuds they felt through the floorboards. Finally the car skidded to a stop, dark smoke wafting from its grill. Landsaw's door was stuck against the bank and he crawled toward Julie, sending her out first. They stood in the rain in the center of the road and watched the motionless figure behind them, indifferent to the storm that drenched it.

"Is he dead?" Landsaw asked.

"I don't know," Julie said.

"Should I turn him over?" Landsaw asked. "What if he has a broken back or something? I forget what the right thing to do is."

Julie watched the body and Landsaw approached it. Lang's corpse was askew on his side, his legs in disarray.

"Okay, yes, he's dead," Landsaw said.

Landsaw edged the body over onto its back and he jumped when Lang's blank countenance turned up toward him. Blood ran from the dead man's face with the rain, and for a long time Landsaw watched it run.

THIRTY-EIGHT

The sun broke in a splinter out over the sea, its light preceding its form upon the water in black and blue pockets of dawn. Whitecaps splashed up in the wind and palms shook on the shore. Clouds cleared a path of morning sky on the water and Sunny paddled through it. Below him, surgeonfish considered an ancient sea grass meadow, while on the nearby rocks, sanderlings worked at algae in the foreground of Oahu's southern shore.

A small wave swelled, the size Sunny had been waiting for. It rose long and evenly until it broke in a crisp cascade. Another surfer dropped into it, adulterating its perfection, though surfing a long and flawless ride. Sunny waited for another one to arise, but the missed opportunity of the first wave rendered the rest of them inadequate, and after a while he paddled back in.

At home, Eileen Spitzer was moving from room to room in the ritual morning rush.

"Eat those muffins you bought," she called from the bedroom. "They're going stale and I'm not touching them."

The weight of the trial that led to Landsaw's ten-year sentencing had further accelerated Sunny and Spitzer's already burgeoning codependence. The press had churned the otherwise solemn proceedings into a national spectacle, with an encampment of media busses clogging the narrow streets beyond St. Bart's.

"How was it?" Spitzer asked Sunny as she ironed down a renegade curl before the bathroom mirror.

"Nice for a while," Sunny said.

"Then what?" Spitzer asked.

"Then nothing," Sunny said. "Then it wasn't. Then it was over."

"At least there were waves," she said, returning to the kitchen where Sunny stood considering the plastic bag of muffins.

He took one out and slipped a corner of it into his mouth before committing, its preservatives, which Spitzer now shunned, having secured its flavor.

"There is that," Sunny said.

Spitzer had given her notice not long after accepting an equivalent position at a Honolulu gallery of lesser stature but of greater integrity. Sunny was not inculpable in the decision, and the bureau agreed to transfer the surfing detective from the city to the beach. The catch was his having to trade art crimes for less interesting fare, namely unearthing mainland fugitives who had fled to Hawaii to reinvent themselves in South Pacific splendor.

Sunny and Spitzer's house was a yellow bungalow set among palms and gardens of tropical flowers, which the neophyte greenthumbs pruned and pampered feverishly on the weekends. The orchids worked on their own mysterious schedule and the plumeria blossomed year-round.

THIRTY-NINE

Julie could not name precisely what it was that she disliked about San Francisco. She knew part of her contempt drew from the contemporary state of the city's once-renegade spirit, now confined to honorary street names and North Beach museums. From her perch on Nob Hill, she felt her own family endemic to the blame. She told herself that if she had she not earned the only job she had wanted, that she would be someplace else entirely, though she had no idea of where that might be.

Landsaw had gleaned the general topography of her life from their limited correspondences while he was away. Their early rounds of letters had been labored. Landsaw was embarrassed; Julie was, too. Their writing would cease for long periods, and their written voices never found the ease they had known. But when he called her from Ruth's, they regressed immediately into their familiar repartee, and Julie invited him to California in the fall.

"I wouldn't want my being there to cause any friction or anything," Landsaw had told her.

"It would honestly be a small miracle if it could," Julie said.

At his layover in Detroit, Landsaw considered turning back or taking a connecting flight elsewhere. He felt watched and checked his clothes repeatedly for indicators that he was anything but a civilian. On the plane he watched the floor of pink clouds beneath him. His luggage was the first bag to slide down the chute at SFO, and at the taxi stand, the first cab waiting was his.

He watched the brown hills out the window, bare above the low rows of pink and white stucco homes. A train moving alongside the highway outpaced the taxi and disappeared beyond them. As they drew toward the city he read the bright billboards advertising electronics he did not understand. He saw the Coit Tower and pictured its murals, cocooned and spiraling up the stairwell.

His motel was called the Seaway and was in a neighborhood his driver told him was called Cow Hollow. Few buildings were higher than two stories and the twin tops of the Golden Gate Bridge rose above a car wash outside his bay-facing window. His room was on the second floor, above a courtyard, where clay pots held pointed yucca, bulbous cacti, and an enormous banana tree.

Leaving his room after settling in, Landsaw encountered a group of young women from the room next to his, spilling out onto the shared balcony. Flutes of champagne suggested a bachelorette party. Holding a glass, barefoot, and followed by her flock to the wrought iron railing for pictures, the bride-to-be approached Landsaw.

"Will you take this?" she asked him, handing Landsaw a camera. "If you can't fit Beth in it's fine."

"Cunt," said the girl who Landsaw guessed was Beth.

The girls laughed and Landsaw lined up the shot before pressing the button he assumed to be the right button. The party dispersed and filed back into their room while the bride retrieved the camera from Landsaw.

"I'm getting married," she told him.

"That's wonderful," Landsaw said.

"We're celebrating that," she said.

"Congratulations," he said.

She intensified her eyes toward him and smiled suggestively, meanwhile letting her fingers linger for a moment on his as he handed back the camera. She then stepped backwards into the room slowly and closed the door, behind which her party's jubilance erupted.

Landsaw walked out into the dusk and found a corner restaurant stationed halfway up a hill. He sat at the crowded bar and ate clams casino overwhelmed by garlic. He tempered his wine and talked with the bartender, who had recently been east to ski. Landsaw chased a complimentary cognac with a rich espresso and savored its dark notes engaging with the lingering spices of his meal. Above the bar hung a wall-length painting in lieu of a mirror, an abstraction with rich reds and Spanish yellow invaded by a supernatural green.

Outside, the night had fallen and the famous fog set in. Landsaw crossed the street to a bar where a band was playing. The band was dressed in cowboy regalia and performing a twanged out take on "In the Evening When the Sun Goes Down." Peanut shells littered the hardwood floor and a young couple swung each other around the crowded barroom. They were dressed for the band, with the woman wearing a polka dot dress cut short and the man in a bandana, boots, and pearl-buttoned shirt tucked into blue jeans adorned with a gunslinger's buckle.

"They're too much, aren't they?" an older woman asked Landsaw.

She was standing at the bar watching the couple execute a practiced-looking dip routine.

"I sure can't do that anymore," she told Landsaw.

The band dropped into "Miserlou," bringing the audience together into an amoeboid tangle. The guitar player entered the orb and the woman next to Landsaw grabbed Landsaw's hand and led him in, leaving him rushing to set his beer back on the bar before he was dragged amongst the writhing mob of dancers. The guitarist performed various tricks of tremolo on muted strings, chopping at the far provinces of the neck to elicit steely pangs of snarled out notes. Landsaw's dance partner ducked below a bridge of arms and entered the inner circle, where she whirled in abandon. The bandleader turned to signal the rhythm section, and with an only slightly perceivable four-count they found the refrain to which they added a cowboy-call chorus and finished the first set.

By midnight, the crowd had bulged to capacity and Landsaw was drunk on his new friend's generosity, if not drained by her battering lessons in the bolero, the Havana Rhumba, and the simple do-si-do. She took off for the restroom while the costumed couple slow danced to a western swing number. Landsaw slipped out through the front. The night was cool and misty, with a sleepy aura engulfing the closed cafés and soft lights spread out on the city's distant hills. Across the way he saw the bartender from earlier lighting a cigarette. Landsaw crossed the street to join him.

"Good time?" the bartender asked.

"Good band," Landsaw said. "But I danced for my drinks."

"Janet?" the bartender asked, inhaling.

"Possibly," Landsaw said. "Sounds right."

"She's a holdover from the old days," the bartender said. "Whenever that was."

Through the barroom windows Landsaw was watching the band finish when Janet came out and scanned the sidewalk up and down, no doubt looking for Landsaw.

The bartender guided him a step back into the shadows, and she soon took off on-foot down the hill.

"Which way am I going?" Landsaw asked. "Cow Hollow?"

The bartender pointed down toward where Janet had gone.

"Might want to give it a minute," he said. "But it's Broadway to Van Ness, take a right and then a left on Lombard."

The cowboy couple came out through the doors and were engaged in an argument. The man left and stormed uphill, looking ridiculous to be so angry in his outfit.

"Happy trails," the bartender said to Landsaw.

He snuffed out his cigarette and turned back into the restaurant to finish closing. Landsaw watched the cowgirl standing alone and beginning to cry. He crossed the street and stood beside her, unsure as to whether he should comfort her, or if such a gesture might warrant a swing in the mouth from her fringe and rhinestone purse.

"Are you alright?" he said.

She began to cry harder then, each wail increasing in volume and intensity as she leaned into Landsaw's arms, which had not been particularly ready to receive her.

"I can bring you home?" Landsaw offered. "I mean to where you live? I think your boyfriend went that way?"

"He's not my boyfriend," she sobbed into Landsaw's sleeve. "We're married."

"Okay," Landsaw said. "Husband then. Can I take you up there?"

She turned to look up at Landsaw, her face swollen with tears.

"He doesn't want me there," she said.

"I'm sure that's not true," Landsaw said. "Everyone's been drinking. It's late and..."

"That's right," she said. "It is late. Too late."

She continued crying into his shoulder until a clap of boots approached them and one arm pulled the woman off of Landsaw while the other hit below his left eye. Landsaw did not remember falling, though he did remember watching from the ground as the cowboy and his wife walked away, arm-in-arm, up the hill. Landsaw lay there a moment to recover and soon heard more footsteps. He readied himself to accept assistance, but when none came, he turned and saw Janet stepping around him, a paper plate of pizza in her hands.

"Serves you right, asshole," she said, passing him by.

Landsaw worked himself to his feet and abandoned his plan to walk back, hailing a Checker Cab instead. At the Seaway, he stood outside his door fishing his pockets for his key. The clay tiles of the courtyard reflected the moonlight. Noises of amorous thrill came muffled through the door next door, and Landsaw wished them well.

FORTY

Clouds with no distinct beginning or end hung fortified against the prospect of a sunny day. In the park, quiet roads wound through quiet meadows and stands of large palms and blue gum eucalyptus framed a California pastoral. There were footpaths edging calm ponds reflecting the tops of city buildings on either side. There were grassy slopes and stables for horses, busy with the noise of morning chores. And there were Landsaw and Julie, walking along the rims of casting pools, which lay flat and still, the gridlines painted on the bottom of each one catching and holding a tenuous green glow through the otherwise deep and dark blue water. Landsaw had met Julie outside of the museum where she worked.

"I don't suppose they even let you in these things anymore," she had joked.

Her hair, shorter now, stirred in wind that Landsaw could not see.

"So are you alright and everything?" she asked him. "I mean is that even okay to ask?"

"Of course," Landsaw said. "It was more strange than anything. I guess it still doesn't feel like it was real."

"You were there a long time," she said.

"Not so long if you think about it," Landsaw said. "Just a third of my life up until now. And if I live twice what I've lived so far, which shouldn't be a problem, it will only be a sixth of my life. If I live three times as long, which I find feasible, it will have only been about one ninth. I just need to make sure the other eight decades make up for it."

"I guess so," she said.

"But my youth?" he said.

"What?" she said.

"Are you not saying 'But your youth?' or something like that?"

Julie smiled.

"I guess so," she said.

"What did I miss?" Landsaw asked. "Was it all they say it is?"

"Not really," she said. "But I might have done it wrong."

"You got off to a pretty strange start," Landsaw said. "Which I do apologize for."

"Don't do that," Julie said.

"I don't feel older yet anyway," Landsaw said. "I mean do you? What's to stop me from being young now?"

"From the looks of your eye, Landsaw, you're not doing so great with that," Julie said. "What was her name, anyway?"

"I didn't catch it," he said. "She was crying and I—"

"Alright Landsaw," Julie said. "I don't need to know."

They stopped beneath a spruce tree and watched its mirrored copy on the slow warp of the pool's surface. A cherry blossom floated out into the middle of the tree's reflection.

"What are you going to do?" Julie asked Landsaw. "I mean generally."

"I got a job," Landsaw said. "Collecting money at the door of a bar where they have music. And there's an apartment above it that I'm moving into. We've been there actually. The bar I mean. You and me."

"You're going to live above a bar?" she asked him.

"It's maybe better than it sounds," he said. "They just tell you to get a job, so that's what I did."

Julie looked at her watch without meaning to and snapped her hand back into her coat pocket.

"Sorry," Landsaw said. "I shouldn't keep you."

"Stop," she said. "You're not."

"Don't get fired on my account," he said. "I mean unless you want to. I understand that it might be tempting to leave everything behind and come live with me above a bar."

Julie smiled and reached for Landsaw's hand.

"This is okay?" he said.

"For now it is," she said.

They walked awhile without speaking.

"The museum world is pretty disappointing," Julie said finally.

"Disappointing how?" Landsaw asked.

"I thought it might be about art," she said. "But it's just about money, and how we can get more of it, even when we have more than we know what to do with."

"You didn't know that?" Landsaw said.

"Neither did you, Landsaw," she said. "What about your art? Did you paint?"

"I didn't not," Landsaw said. "But nothing spectacular. How about you?"

"No," she said. "I could blame it on becoming a mom and life and all, but I think I just realized one day that I wasn't very good. And the investment to get good didn't seem worth the pretty minimal reward."

"What would the pretty minimal reward be?" Landsaw asked.

"Probably nothing," Julie said. "I could have walked around smugly knowing that I could paint a super convincing horse."

They walked on and came to a stone retaining wall off the porch of a shuttered fishing lodge and sat watching the park play out before them. A man in a wool hat walked a small dog. A runner passed by in short orange shorts.

"So I'm going to ask you," Julie said. "But before I do, I want to make sure that all of what happened is okay to talk about. I mean I don't want to undo anything you worked on in therapy or counseling or something like that."

"I'm a dangerous criminal," Landsaw said. "I could fly off the handle at any moment."

"Shut up, Landsaw," Julie said. "So, I've always wondered, what happened with your painting?"

"Which one?" Landsaw said.

"What do you mean which one?" Julie said. "The fake."

"Which fake?" Landsaw said.

"The one you replaced the painting with at the museum," Julie said. "What do you mean which fake?"

"That one's probably still in evidence or something," Landsaw said. "Or else they destroyed it. The other was in Lang's car when, you know."

"What other?" Julie said. "The painting they found in Lang's car was the original. The one you stole and gave to him?"

"Nope," Landsaw said. "That was mine, too. I thought you knew?"

"Are you kidding?" Julie said. "Nobody knows that. I mean, right?"

"I guess not then," Landsaw said.

"Holy shit, Landsaw," Julie said. "That's like a pretty famous painting, you know. It goes on tour and everything."

"Interesting," Landsaw said. "It's had more of a life than I've had."

Julie watched Landsaw.

"But," she said.

"I don't know," Landsaw said.

"Know what?"

"The original," Landsaw said. "Is that what you were going to ask?"

"You really don't know?"

Landsaw shrugged.

"I lost track," Landsaw said. "I used to have it. My mom moved a bunch of stuff around when she started going to Florida. It probably got tossed."

"Holy shit, Landsaw," Julie said. "Couldn't you get in trouble?"

"I don't think so," Landsaw said. "I mean, part of my sentence was for stealing the painting. Or picture? I'm not sure I can serve that twice. Double indemnity or whatever."

"Double jeopardy," Julie said.

"Sure," Landsaw said.

"But—" Julie started.

"It's alright," Landsaw said. "And I really am sorry, Julie."

"Shut up, Landsaw," she said.

She let her head rest lightly on his shoulder as they sat.

"What if someone sees you?" Landsaw asked.

"It doesn't matter," Julie said.

They were quiet for a moment and birds called from tree to tree.

"I remember you used to think that whichever way something turned out, that it was just as well as every other possibility," Julie said. "I guess I'm wondering if you still think that."

"I'm not sure I ever really thought that," Landsaw said. "It was probably just something I said."

Julie nodded and checked her wrist again, this time in earnest.

"Probably time, then," Landsaw said.

He stood and Julie unclasped his hand.

"What are these pools for anyway?" he asked.

189

"Fly fishing," she said.

"I don't see any fish," he said.

Julie craned her neck out toward the pools.

"They stock them sometimes," she said. "In the spring I think."

"Kind of seems like cheating," Landsaw said. "Catching stocked fish."

"How's that?" she asked.

"Because you're learning to catch stocked fish," he said. "Not real ones."

"Stocked fish are real fish," she said.

"Arguably," he said.

They walked back toward the museum and stood on the broad steps in the sun to say goodbye. Pigeons idled around them, pecking at the ground.

"Tell your mom hi?" Julie said.

"I will," Landsaw said. "She's boarding up the house right now before driving down to Florida. This new snowbird thing is weird to me. I think she's met someone she isn't telling me about yet."

"Couldn't have expected her to wait around forever," Julie said.

"Certainly she deserves better," Landsaw said.

Back upstairs, Julie sat in the relative quiet of her office and replayed her walk with Landsaw in her head, silently amending their conversation. She considered the excitement that they were the only two people on earth who knew something. She was considering this when someone knocked on her office door.

"Yeah," she said.

An intern opened it and held up a cardboard tube.

"Someone left this for you," the intern said.

He placed it on her desk while Julie turned to her computer to pretend she had been busier than she was.

"Great," she said. "Thanks Isaac."

"Iván," the intern said.

"What?" Julie said.

"My name," the intern said. "It's Iván."

"Oh," she said. "Right. And what is this again?"

She gestured at the tube impatiently.

"I don't know," Iván said. "It just has your name on it."

Julie picked it up and began removing the packing tape. Iván was waiting in the doorway and Julie stopped to look up at him.

"Anything else?" she said.

"Uh, nope," Iván said.

"Great," Julie said.

She smiled at Iván until he walked backwards through the door and closed it behind him.

Julie continued working the tape off until finally she plucked loose the plastic cap. She held the package sideways and peered in, carefully as though she were checking a trap. A canvas was coiled tightly to the sides with a brief note inside the center's empty space.

FORTY-ONE

Gas lines off, pilot lights out, and water mains stopped and drained, Ruth toured the house once more in a round of triple certainly that even the most persistent of winter weather would not breach the aging frame. Anything of serious value had been packed neatly into the Coachmen; everything else she reminded herself she could lose. Ron, standing in the leaf-littered lawn, ran down the rest of the checklist: electricity, cut; refrigerator, defrosted; windows, locked; plants, those not adopted by Ron, abandoned to the compost. Beds were made and sinks and showers scrubbed clean. Patio furniture, candles, and decorations had been dismantled and stored beneath the porch. The gardens were covered and the mower, its battery removed, she had locked in the shed.

Ruth stood with Ron and gauged the height of a theoretical storm.

"The place could be buried," he said. "You're fine."

It was early and the clouds were thick among the trees. Ruth chinned up at a leaning sugar maple near the house.

"I should have cut that one down," she said.

"It won't go yet," Ron said.

Ruth climbed into the Coachmen and started it. The engine sounded young again. She rolled down the window and pulled out carefully. In a moment, Ron was a waving fragment of her rearview. She negotiated the big curve slowly and feathered the Coachmen off of the hill, coasting down into the day from her perch in the low-hanging sky.

Photo by Luke Awtry

John Y. Flanagan lives in Starksboro, Vermont. *Fakists* is his first novel.

CPSIA information can be obtained
at www.ICGtesting.com
Printed in the USA
BVHW041700180423
662583BV00020B/310